GW00806389

PIERCING THE VEIL

JACQUELINE FULLERTON

PIERCING THE VEIL

A. P. Lee & Co., Ltd.
Columbus, OH

AP Lee & Co.
PO Box 340292
Columbus, OH 43234
"Evolving mankind, one book at a time."

Copyright © 2009 by Jacqueline Fullerton
First Edition: February 2009

Cover and book design: Gwyn Kennedy Snider

Library of Congress Control Number: 2008929076

ISBN-13: 978-1-934482-03-2
ISBN-10: 1-934482-03-X

ACKNOWLEDGEMENTS

No author does it alone. I am fortunate to have many friends and family members who offer me constant support and encouragement: my husband and friend, Tom; my friends Nanci and Sharon; my family; my Editor Beth; and many, many others I am privileged to know.

PIERCING THE VEIL

1

"Tim's a snake. Be careful, Anne. This man will stop at nothing to get what he wants."

Anne sat up in bed. A shiver ran through her at hearing her father's voice. She wiped the sleep from her eyes and looked around. Slivers of light fell across the bed, illuminating the empty place next to her. She longed for Jason, wished he was there to comfort her. *Am I going crazy? How could my father have spoken to me? He's been dead for two years.*

Anne's father watched as she fell back to sleep. Not even death had dulled his memories of their time together, from the day she was born and he first held her, to watching her leaving for her senior prom. How did she grow up so fast? They had planned to practice law together. He hadn't planned on dying from a massive heart attack at sixty-two. He wanted so much to give her a hug and kiss her goodnight. But those days were over. He recalled how he had helped his little girl–teaching her to ride a bike, showing her how to hold a baseball bat, assisting her with math homework. Now he needed her help. He had been trying for weeks to get her attention. He thought he could reach her through her dreams. Nothing seemed to be working. He had to find a way to communicate with her. And soon.

•••••••

Tim Sherman sat in the dark, staring at his computer. It was after 9:00 p.m., and everyone else had left for the day. His excitement mounted. He was making the final deposit into his offshore account. He had set the plan in motion several years before, when he began draining money from the company into his own private account. And he had done it under the eyes of his soon-to-be ex-wife Isabelle. With this last deposit he would have a little over $10 million. He began to hyperventilate as he entered the account number, one deliberate keystroke at a time. He couldn't afford to make a mistake. Inhaling and exhaling fully, he experienced the exhilaration of his efforts. He licked his lips. His fat, sweaty hand hovered over the keyboard.

"Tim, darlin', are you still in there?"

Sherman shot back in his chair. He recognized the voice of his Office Manager, Stephanie Burke, calling from the front office. She switched on the hall lights.

"Damn," he wondered, "what is she doing here?"

Stephanie was a minor misstep in his methodically laid-out plan. She could, however, become a major misstep if he didn't handle it right. He took a deep breath and put on a pleasant voice.

"One minute, sweetie, I have to finish something." He pressed "Enter" and watched the wire transfer jump from the company account to his own. Beads of perspiration gathered on his forehead as he watched the money disappear from the company coffers.

He needed only a few seconds to be sure that the transfer was complete. Then he could savor his accomplishment. He logged into his account and pressed the balance button: $10,132,689.00. *Transfer complete.* He smirked. His future was secure. He imagined Isabelle's shock when she discovered that he was long gone–with all their money. He logged out and shut down his computer. His heart raced. He would have to be very careful. Timing was everything.

A successful businessman in his late fifties, Tim Sherman had started a financial advisory company over twenty years ago with his wife Isabelle. Tim had always felt smug about his success. He had been the one with the talent and the expertise. He had built the company alone. He acknowledged that Isabelle's money and connections had given him the start, but that was minor compared to his genius. Now, in the middle of a messy divorce settlement, she was accusing him of squirreling away money. He, of course, denied it. Everything would have been perfect if she hadn't gotten the idiotic idea to divorce him before he could follow through with his plan. Now he would have to play along through court proceedings for a few more days. Then he would disappear and never again have to bother with Isabelle, Stephanie, or the business.

Stephanie walked into his office, startling him. "There you are, Tim, darlin'. What are you doing here so late anyway? I called your cell phone. Why didn't you answer, sugar?" She purred as she rounded his desk. "I was so worried, so I thought I would come find you." He could see her panty lines under her tight skirt.

Her voice grated, sending a chill through him. He swallowed. *I have to fake this a little while longer.* He and Stephanie had been having an affair for over a year now. One in a long line of affairs he'd had during his marriage. He had never allowed himself to get involved with anyone at work–until Stephanie. But he found her irresistible. The sex was absolutely beyond anything he had ever experienced. And the gratification of having sex so close to Isabelle's watchful eye heightened his pleasure. He and Stephanie had sex in his office every chance they got. He felt powerful when he could buzz her into his office on a whim. Seconds later she'd be locking the door and unbuttoning her blouse to reveal her remarkably firm breasts. When he knew there were clients waiting outside his door, his passion grew. Their little dance excited Tim, made him feel like a young man again.

As had happened with his many conquests before Stephanie, Sherman grew restless and bored after six or so months. He had been poised to fire Stephanie when she stumbled onto his offshore activities. He had been careless one night and Stephanie turned out to be far more astute than he would have imagined. She now had the account number and password. Rather than panic, Sherman turned it to his advantage, enlisting her help in exchange for a promise that the two of them would spend the rest of their lives together. Since she had access to the accounting books, it was easy for them to cover their tracks. Stephanie was so gullible; it was almost too easy. Like taking candy from a baby. He felt certain she swallowed his story that they would be together after his divorce became final. Silly woman. Tim had already hatched a plan to eliminate her. He would disappear before anyone had a clue.

"I'm finishing up some business, sweetheart," he said. Sherman could sound charming and persuasive when he had to. He turned to see Stephanie standing over him. She straddled him while unbuttoning his shirt. He knew he had to keep the game going a little while longer. Then he could be rid of her for good. She started to fondle him and he responded. He groped her breast with his thick fingers while she covered his mouth with hot, wet kisses. "Not even a fool would turn down pleasure," he thought. His hand crawled up her warm thigh.

2

Anne managed to pull herself out of bed after hitting the snooze alarm only twice. She'd had an unusually restless night. Ever since she had been assigned as court reporter to the Sherman divorce case she had been plagued with nightmares. She would awaken several times a night, drenched in sweat, after hearing her father warning her about Tim Sherman. Her father's death from a heart attack two years before had devastated Anne. She missed him daily but had, over time, managed to encapsulate the loss. Why was she dreaming about him now? And what could she possibly do about Tim Sherman? Sure, it unnerved her to see Tim and Isabelle Sherman at each other's throats over money. They had been longtime acquaintances of her parents. Maybe thoughts of their disquieting relationship had paired with her overactive imagination and manifested in the troublesome dreams. *What else could it possibly be?* She scratched her head and headed to the shower. If she didn't dawdle, she could still stop at Starbuck's and make it to the office on time. She might even indulge in a pecan sweet roll dripping with icing. Let's face it; she was a gnawer who needed to chew on something. She deserved a treat after the night she had endured. With that delicious thought hanging on her lips, she moved into warp speed.

"Way to go, girl." She gave herself an imaginary high-five half an hour later, picked up her purse, and left her apartment. She was greeted in the hall by Mrs. Myer's well-fed tabby, Aristotle, who strutted from behind a pile of papers in the corner. He shot her a look of arrogance that only a cat can deliver. Pure arrogance.

"Good morning, Aristotle." She kneeled down and rubbed him behind the ears. He responded by rubbing against her, then shifted into purr drive and demanded more attention.

"Sorry, old boy, gotta run." She scooted out the door and focused on a Starbuck's—a hot, steamy Caramel Macchiato. She had earned it.

The bus stop was two blocks from Anne's

apartment. She enjoyed the short walk. It helped her clear her head. Her late model Mazda was sitting outside her apartment but she preferred taking the bus. Parking at the courthouse was a major source of aggravation–and expensive. Riding the bus was an affordable hassle-free alternative. "Avoid the Fuss, Ride the Bus," she whispered under her breath as she crossed the street.

Anne lived in a part of town that could best be described as old world European. Her apartment was one of four that had been carved from a stately, red brick home. Most of the buildings in the neighborhood had been built prior to World War II and now housed artists, students, and young professionals. Anne approached the bus stop and checked her watch. *Still time for her macchiato and calorie-laden sweet roll.* She took her place at the bus stop with the other riders, nondescript except for an older man who stood apart from the others. Anne watched him as he eyed the bank across the street. Maybe he had exhausted his Social Security checks and was living on cat food and water. He needed a bank heist to survive. The bus pulled up, interrupting her reverie. The story dissolved as she paid her fare and found a seat. The bank robber followed behind her. He smiled as he passed. She noticed a Wall Street Journal tucked under the arm of his tweed jacket.

"Oh well," she mused, "so much for the desperate bank robber."

The bus resumed its rhythmic journey toward downtown Brecksville, a small midwestern town that depended on two main employers for its livelihood—the courthouse and Compton University. Anne settled back and let her mind wander. At twenty-six, she was single and enrolled in Compton's law school. She attended classes at night. To support herself she worked part-time as a court reporter. She loved her job, especially the drama and intrigue that haunts all courthouses.

Since her father's death, Anne had felt abandoned and lonely. She had a loving family and friends, but without her dad, a piece of her was missing. James Marshall had been a professor of criminal law at Compton and one of the reasons she had enrolled in law school. After his retirement from Jones and Schwartz, the town's most prestigious law firm, her dad had created an office in the garage next to their home. He had always dreamed of taking on pro bono "underdog" cases. A formidable, yet kind man, he resembled Jimmy Stewart. Nobody ever questioned his passion for the law. He had been thrilled when Anne decided to follow in his footsteps. She had planned to enter his practice and eventually take it over, but his death at sixty-two closed that door. Anne still felt the pain deep in her soul. And, here she was, dreaming about him every night. The last few days, she had smelled his pipe tobacco on waking. What was that about? Was she having some sort of breakdown?

Enough melancholy, she thought, shaking her head to dismiss the troublesome thoughts. The bus stopped at the courthouse. Anne got off and strode purposefully to the kiosk in front of the building. Longingly she eyed the pecan roll. Her mouth watered as she imagined the taste of creamy frosting studded with pecan bits. If she gave in now she would probably pay for it the next time she got on the scale. *Be strong, Anne.* She heaved a heavy sigh. "I'll have a Tall Caramel Macchiato with low fat milk, please." She emphasized "low fat milk" to feel virtuous. Coffee would have to satisfy her sweet tooth for now. Seconds later she inhaled the pleasing aroma and took a sip. She envisioned Snoopy, floating above his doghouse, ears twisted, feet flapping, in absolute ecstasy. "Ah, all is right with the world."

The courthouse was buzzing. She opened the door to her office, hung up her jacket, and unloaded her briefcase. Checking the day's schedule, she noticed a delay in the Sherman divorce case. A chill ran up her spine. *That's strange.* But she had to admit that the entire Sherman case was strange. She would be glad when it ended. Maybe then the nightmares would stop.

In place of the Sherman case, she would be covering a contested divorce; a couple with plenty of money and no children. Both wanted custody of their poodle, Precious. She smirked. *How ironic. The only precious thing left in their marriage was the dog.* The rest of the schedule looked routine. She would have plenty of time to transcribe the testimony and get to law school by early afternoon.

On her way to Courtroom C Anne spotted Tim Sherman walking with his attorneys. When she saw him her heart rate quickened. "Tim's a snake. Don't trust him," her father had said. She couldn't fathom what the warning meant, but every nerve in her body tingled. She ducked into an alcove until Sherman was out of sight, then made her way toward the courtroom. She spied Jason Perry, her boyfriend, and a smile crept across her face. They planned to marry when she finished law school in four years. She couldn't wait to be with him all the time.

Jason was a diligent, brilliant Assistant District Attorney who, like every other young civil servant, worked long hours juggling an impossible caseload. A year older than Anne, he had dusty blond hair, piercing blue eyes, and a smile that would melt any heart. Anne thought he could have been Robert Redford's stand-in.

Anne and Jason made a striking couple. Anne had short dark hair that curled around her face, and flashing hazel eyes. Even with a light dusting of makeup, some freckles peaked through. Anne and Jason had known each other since high school. After graduating from college, Jason had gone to law school while Anne vacillated between graduate school and a career. She called to him.

Jason turned. He returned her wave and tapped his watch. He held an imaginary sandwich and bit into it, which told her they would meet at lunch.

Anne laughed and nodded in recognition. She pushed the large mahogany doors and went in. Her table was located in front of the judge's bench. She pulled her memo-scriber out of its case, loaded the steno paper, and slid in the battery. Satisfied that all was in working order, she waited for court to be called to order. She glanced at the two tables where the plaintiff and defendant sat, flanked by their well-paid lawyers. It distressed her that two people who were once in love could end up enemies. She felt certain that the animosity had more to do with bruised egos. She had seen many similar cases. Both parties seemed intent on inflicting pain on their partner. Her mind drifted. She visualized Missus catching Mister with his secretary in a passionate embrace late one night. Or, tired of the long hours Mister put in at the office, Missus wanted out. Maybe she planned to run off to Rio de Janeiro with their pool boy and Precious. Here, "'till death do us part" boiled down to a husband and wife fighting over a ten-pound poodle.

"So sad," Anne thought. "I'll never let that happen." Without thinking she pulled out a pencil and sunk her teeth into it. It was one of those annoying habits she had developed early in life. Anne deduced that her mother had taken away her pacifier too soon. Whatever the reason, she chewed when she was bored, when she was tired, and when she was nervous. As a result, her desk was cluttered with remnants of once respectable pencils.

Judge Franklin walked into the courtroom, drawing Anne back to the real world. Everyone rose. The bailiff had called the courtroom to order.

Anne tapped at the keys and struggled to stay awake during the proceedings. A little before noon, the Judge proposed that the couple share custody of Precious. Everyone agreed. Anne wished all cases could be settled as amiably and equitably. She grabbed her stacks of steno paper and headed to the lunchroom where she grabbed a salad and a bottle of water. She joined Jason. He was munching on a tuna salad sandwich and frowning over papers.

"Tough morning?" she asked.

He gathered the papers and shoved them into his briefcase.

"Not really, just tough clients," he smiled. "How was your morning?"

"Uneventful," she shrugged. "If we ever get a dog, let's decide ownership from the start."

Jason looked a little dismayed. "Fair enough, but if it's a manly dog like a Labrador Retriever, I claim ownership. No arguments. If it's a fluffy foo-foo dog like a poodle, it's all yours."

Anne laughed. "I think I'll finish early enough to review my cases one more time for Property Law tonight."

"Ugh! I have vivid memories of Professor Craft's Socratic method that still give me chills, but I know you will ace it. Need any help?"

"No thanks. My study group meets right before class."

"Thank God. As you know, Property Law was not my favorite subject."

"You don't find title disputes and water rights absolutely fascinating?" she teased.

"Afraid not." Jason looked at his watch. "I have to run. Pre-trial conference. Call me when you get home. Love you." He leaned over and gave her a kiss on the forehead, tossed his leftovers in the trash, and disappeared down the hall. Anne smiled. She loved him so much. She felt a warm glow flood her body.

Anne breezed through an afternoon of minor hearings and walked the few blocks to school.

Small and prestigious, Compton had turned out some of the best legal minds in the country. Jason was fiercely proud to be a graduate and Anne looked forward to someday holding the same honor. The law school had been constructed in

1895. The building's facade was weathered grey stone and the windows and doorways were covered with thick ivy. The heating and air conditioning left something to be desired, but the building's Ivy League charm more than made up for the seasonal inconveniences.

Anne climbed the front steps and transitioned from working girl to student. Academia had always appealed to her. She didn't care if she became the oldest night student in the Guinness Book of World Records.

Anne greeted her classmates and headed to the basement lunchroom, a misnomer for a cavern full of vending machines. She turned the corner and spotted two members of her study group deep in discussion. As she approached, she heard Bryan Knightly and Maria Gomez O'Malley arguing over a case. Bryan was an accountant at a local CPA firm. He and his wife, Celia, had been married eight years and had two adorable kids. Bryan had always wanted to be an attorney, but his father had insisted on accounting. "Always need accountants," his father had said. Now, with his wife's support, Bryan was fulfilling his own dream. He justified the move by stating unequivocally, "an accountant who can also defend his client is an even more valuable commodity."

Maria was a homicide detective, one of the first Hispanic females promoted to that position. She'd won accolades for her service to the force. At the police academy, Maria had fallen in love with and married Shane O'Malley, a red-headed Irishman also assigned to homicide. Maria had entered law school before they had any children.

Bryan and Maria stopped in mid-sentence to greet Anne. She pulled a chair over.

Maria turned to Anne. "You have to agree that the court was obviously biased in rendering the majority opinion in Metzger versus Denton."

Bryan cut her off. "Bias has nothing to do with it. The facts speak for themselves."

Anne held up her hands. "Stop! I'm an innocent bystander," she laughed. "And, besides, Bryan, you will never out argue Maria." She winked at Maria. "It's not even vaguely possible."

Before Bryan could protest, Anne pleaded, "Please, please help me with some of these cases. I dread what will happen if I fall into Professor Craft's clutches unprepared."

"Don't we all." Bryan said.

Anne heard approaching footsteps and looked up. "Hi guys," she greeted Clark and John, the other members of the study group. Clark Meadows was an insurance executive with one of the big health insurance companies and John Karr had a computer consulting business. The two had met in undergraduate school and had never separated. Clark's employer had encouraged him to get his law degree. John thought it would be useful in his business, so they enrolled together. Anne was pleased with her group and the ease with which they worked together. The group was her lifeline.

A little before six they grabbed their books and walked to class. At exactly 6:00 p.m., Professor Craft walked in. The classroom door slammed behind him as he swaggered over to his elevated desk and pulled out his books. He had the reputation of being one of the toughest professors at Compton, failing half his students. He climbed onto his stool, glared at the class, and pounced on his first victim. Anne thanked her lucky stars that he hadn't called on her.

3

Anne walked in the door a little after ten. It had been a long day and she could barely keep her eyes open. She grabbed a bottle of water from the refrigerator and scanned the pantry for a snack. She spotted a bag of Oreo cookies hidden in the corner behind the linguine. That was her emergency supply–"Break Open Only in Case of Emergency." She hesitated, then tucked a bag of low-fat chips under her arm and collapsed on her living room sofa. She picked up the TV remote and clicked through a bunch of reruns. She settled on an old Clint Eastwood movie and set the volume on low. After kicking off her shoes, she curled up under a soft, wooly afghan. Anne reached for the telephone and dialed Jason.

"Hey you."

"Hey you back," he responded. "How was Professor Craft?"

"As lethal as ever," she grimaced. They chatted a few minutes but Anne could no longer suppress a yawn. "As much as I love you, I'm beat."

"I feel your pain. Love you and I will see you in the morning."

After she had hung up, she smiled to herself. Thoughts of Jason, two children, a rose-covered cottage, and happily ever after filled her head as she fell asleep–bag of potato chips in one hand, the remote in the other.

Anne's father watched as she drifted into sleep. He needed to get through to her, but how? He needed something more dramatic.

For the first night in a long time, Anne slept peaceably. The next sound she heard was the opening music for the morning news. She jumped up and looked at the clock. *Great. I'm late.* She showered, dressed and rushed out the door. Aristotle was waiting in the hall, hoping for a morning rub. Anne obliged, then ran to the bus stop.

Half an hour later, checking the schedule, she saw the Sherman case was back on. "Finally, some closure," she thought.

Anne headed for the courtroom. She was stopped by the throng of people shoving to get through the courtroom doors. No doubt most were press jockeying for seats, anxious to capture juicy angles for the evening news. The Shermans were big news in Brecksville. Isabelle Sherman sat on most of the charitable organization boards and Tim Sherman was considered a community leader. Not to mention that Isabelle made certain her accusations were well-known. Anne's sense of excitement mounted. Her pulse raced and she felt a little giddy as she elbowed her way into the room. This is what she loved about the law and her job—drama with a capital D.

Gerard, an openly gay white male in his late thirties, was the bailiff. He wore a pink shirt, tight black pants, and enough bling to set off every metal detector in the courthouse. Most courtrooms required more professional dress, but here in Brecksville everyone was a bit more relaxed, and, being a college town, a lot more tolerant. For all his drama, Gerard was one of the best bailiffs in the courthouse and Judge Johnston's courtroom ran like a well-oiled machine. Paperwork was impeccable and timely. Order was maintained and, bling aside, proper decorum prevailed. Gerard was a decent human being and Anne knew he would do anything for her. She considered him a great and loyal friend.

He looked up at her as she brushed his desk. He smiled and winked. "Girl, are we gonna have a day."

"You know you love it," Anne retorted.

"You got that right." He pushed away from his desk and sashayed into the judge's chambers. A few minutes later, the attorneys, clients in tow, filed into the courtroom. Tim Sherman looked his usual arrogant, defiant self. Though considerably overweight, his trendy thousand-dollar suit camouflaged his bulges. Four attorneys flanked him. Anne recognized the senior partner, Norm Reese. "Ouch," Anne thought. "A real junkyard dog."

Looking confident, Isabelle Sherman was a very attractive woman in her late fifties. She had taken care of herself. The years of beauty treatments and weekend health spas had paid off. Isabelle wore a soft brown, designer suit. Expensive-looking leather heels–probably Manolos–and tasteful, expensive jewelry completed the look.

Anne envied women who could spend that much time—and money—on their looks. She felt lucky to have the time to run a brush through her hair in the morning. She would leave the bling to Gerard. And the hours of self-care to Mrs.

Sherman.

Isabelle Sherman walked past Tim Sherman and his attorneys with an attitude that mesmerized Anne. A posse of attorneys followed her at a respectful distance, through the throng of reporters. Anne spotted Randy Vers, Isabelle's lead attorney. Randy had been a former student and longtime friend of her father's. Her father had taken Randy under his wing, mentoring him and securing a clerkship for him with the firm. It was there that Randy met his wife Ilene, secretary to Anne's father. Anne recalled that her dad had jested that he would never forgive Randy for stealing Ilene. Her dad had been Randy's best man and was the godfather to their sons. Until his death, he had been a surrogate dad to Randy, whose father died when Randy was twelve. Anne felt certain that her father's death had hit Randy almost as hard as it had hit her.

Randy Vers was a partner with Blankenship, Campbell & Germane, a well-respected firm and one of the state's largest. Anne thought it was a coup that Mrs. Sherman had snagged Randy before her husband did. Randy glanced at Anne and gave her a warm smile. She smiled and waved. Randy pulled back the chair for his client.

Anne noticed that the Shermans avoided direct eye contact with each other. They postured to demonstrate more confidence and annoyance than the other. "What a circus," Anne thought. "Wouldn't miss it for the world."

"Anne, he's lying," a voice whispered behind her. "You have to stop him."

That was her father's voice. Anne jerked around to see who had spoken, but no one was there. She glanced around the courtroom. Everyone was occupied. Her skin prickled. She felt as though she had put her finger in a socket. A smell of pipe tobacco filled her nostrils. *Get a grip on yourself.*

She looked across the courtroom where Gerard had returned to his desk. He returned her glance and tapped his head. "You are so right," she thought. "This is crazy. More than you think."

Gerard called the court to attention as Judge Johnston appeared. The Judge peered over the top of his bifocals as he sat down. His stern expression broadcast that he would not tolerate any disruptions. He nodded at Anne who nodded back, indicating she was ready. He asked if both parties were ready to proceed. They said they were, and the curtain rose.

The testimony presented that morning made it

apparent that Mrs. Sherman would have difficulty proving Mr. Sherman had hidden assets. According to the client lists and transaction records, the company was in good financial shape. Yet all the accounting records indicated otherwise. The morning moved at a snail's pace. One accountant after another presented lengthy financial statements. Judge Johnston called for a recess until one o'clock. Anne gathered her transcription and heard Gerard calling her name. She turned to see him scurry up to her.

"Hey, girlfriend, want company for lunch?"

"I'd love it." She took his arm and they made their way to the cafeteria. She looked forward to gossiping with Gerard.

"What do you think of the Shermans?" Gerard asked Anne in a hushed voice. She bit into her tuna fish sandwich. "Do you think he is hiding money? Did you get a look at her Manolos? They are to die for. And that purse must have cost a thousand or more." Gerard munched a cookie.

"I am always suspicious of a successful husband who claims he has no money," Anne replied. "I definitely think he hid it. And I have this nagging feeling that something's not right."

Guesses and conjectures ate up the lunch

break. Anne enjoyed lunching with Gerard because they could indulge their overactive imaginations. It was their little secret. And no harm done.

Gerard called Judge Johnston's court to order at one fifteen. Tim Sherman's attorney put him on the witness stand. Isabelle and her attorneys leaned forward, eager to snap up any tidbit that might help their case.

The questioning was routine.

"Have you disclosed all your assets? Do you have any accounts that were not disclosed? Have you offered this court all of your true and correct financial records?" The answers were predictable. Yes, he had disclosed all his assets. No, he had no accounts that were not disclosed. Yes, he was being complete in his financial records. If opposing counsel were hoping for a slip up, they had to be disappointed. Sherman was a good witness.

At a little after three, Judge Johnston adjourned for the day. The courtroom cleared. The court had agreed to daily transcripts, so Anne made a beeline to her office. According to her calculations, she would have just enough time to transcribe the testimony before class. Her fingers flew. She finished the last page, placed the bound transcripts in the attorney boxes, and rushed out the door.

Going to law school at night was rough, but Anne knew many who had done it and survived. Some had told her it would be like four years in boot camp. No friends, no family, and no social life. She had survived one and a half years and the advice was on target. This semester she had Property Law on Monday, Tax Law on Tuesday, Evidence on Thursday, and then three days in the Law Library reading cases and working on her class outlines. Her study group had become like family. It left little time for Jason. Thank heaven he understood.

Anne grabbed her books and headed for school. Her group assembled and they started their review. The law school program was lockstep, which meant everyone took the same classes through the first three years. She found comfort in knowing that her study group was intact for at least another year and a half.

Tax Law dragged and she had trouble focusing. Professor Spears was not a Socratic teacher, so he presented a succession of cases for the entire three hours. Anne started to chew on the top of her pen, then realized what she was doing and set it down. The last time she had been so careless, she ended up with blue ink all over her mouth. Not attractive. As soon as class ended, Anne raced for the bus. Relief washed over her. Anne liked Tuesdays because she had Wednesdays off. She went through her nightly ritual at home: checked the mail, pitching most of it on her way to the kitchen, switched on the television, then searched the refrigerator. She called Jason. They chatted for about twenty minutes, then said their good nights. She went to her bedroom, changed into sweats, climbed into bed and fell fast asleep.

•••••••

Tim Sherman, feeling even smugger than the day before if that were possible, peered at his bank account. The power and satisfaction he felt were indescribable. He picked up the phone and dialed Stephanie. Time for a little TLC to keep the situation under control.

"Tim, it sounds like things went very well today. A few more days and we're off to a sunny beach. I can almost feel the sand between my toes."

"Now Stephanie, sweetie, remember it's not over

yet. Tomorrow is your big day in court. Remember they will try to trick you. You must stay calm. Think before you answer and don't say anything that will ruin our plans."

"Darlin', you know you can count on me. I know exactly how to handle this."

Sherman's stomach knotted.

4

Anne bolted upright. Another nightmare. Taking deep, even breaths, she tried to focus. The red diodes on her bedside clock read 3:00 a.m. *When will these stop?* Maybe she could shake it off if she got up. She had read somewhere that when you wake in the middle of the night, you should read or go to another room. She walked to the refrigerator and grabbed a bottle of water. Bits and pieces of the dream started coming back to her. She recalled snippets of a conversation with her father about Tim Sherman. She went to her desk for pen and paper. It always helped her to write things down. Returning to bed, she sat cross-legged and reconstructed the dream. She closed her eyes to better concentrate and heard her father's voice fading in and out. *I want to help you Dad, but I don't know what you're telling me. Isabelle Sherman's attorneys are missing something–what?* As hard as she tried, Anne couldn't recall anything other than "offshore account." She sat quietly for a few minutes. Dead end. In frustration, she set aside her notes, drew the covers up and drifted back to sleep.

Anne's father watched in frustration. *Damn. I'm still not getting through.* Then he had an idea.

Something rang, jarring Anne awake. She glanced at the clock: 6:00 a.m. She reluctantly rolled out of bed. In the shower, pieces of her dream flashed back. She heard her dad's voice in her head. "He's lying. He has an offshore account." Nah. That's what she and Gerard had said over lunch. Maybe she was working too hard. A quiet evening with Jason would help.

Leaving her apartment, Anne dismissed the dream and looked around for Aristotle. He was nowhere to be found. Probably out "catting" around, she mused.

At the courthouse she checked in and noticed that the attorneys had already retrieved the previous day's transcripts. On her way to the lunchroom for a cappuccino, someone grabbed her arm and yanked her back into her office. She wriggled around to see it was Isabelle Sherman's attorney, Randy Vers. His jaw was clenched, his face flushed. He slammed the door behind them.

"What in the world is wrong with you?"

She rubbed her arm where it felt bruised. Randy shook a transcript in her face.

"Randy, what's going on?" She had never seen him angry or thought of him as someone to be feared.

"Anne, have you read your transcript? Do you have any idea what you wrote?"

Anne reached for the binder, but he pulled it away.

"What are you talking about? You're not making sense."

"You typed that Mr. Sherman admitted to lying. And that he hid the assets in an offshore account where his wife would never find them. In fact, that entire section is gibberish. It doesn't accurately reflect any of yesterday's testimony. What were you thinking?"

"What?" Anne gasped. She felt pounding in her ears.

"I would never put words in a witness' mouth. There must be some mistake."

Was she awake or dreaming? She prided herself on her accuracy. And her colleagues praised her for it.

"I don't believe you. Is this your idea of a sick joke?"

"Of course not. I came in early and read the transcript. Lucky for you I did. I confiscated all the copies before Mr. Sherman's attorneys could see it. They'd have every right to get you fired." He paused.

Anne's hands trembled. She tried to find her voice but couldn't.

"Anne, as your friend, I'm telling you we need to get to the bottom of this. Immediately." Randy's voice had returned to its normal timbre.

Anne's heart raced. She felt lightheaded.

"I'm going to Judge Johnston's courtroom right now. We need these daily transcripts for cross-examination. I'll ask for a recess until tomorrow. You need time to fix this."

"Give me the transcripts."

He handed them to her and whispered, "You better shred these immediately. I don't know what would happen if Sherman's attorneys saw these libelous accusations." He left abruptly.

Anne looked at the binders in her hand and shook her head. "This is a mistake." She put them on her desk, sat down, and picked up the top copy. She grabbed a pencil and chewed while she read.

She scanned the pages. Everything looked normal. The witnesses' statements, the financial reports, Tim Sherman's testimony. Then she read a paragraph that knocked the wind out of her. At the point when the attorney had asked Mr. Sherman about his hidden account, the testimony did not ring true. According to the transcript, Sherman admitted hiding funds where his wife would never find them. He admitted lying to the court. He admitted falsifying company books.

Anne read quickly through the rest of Sherman's testimony. *How did this happen?* She had been there. She knew what she'd heard. Tim had admitted none of this. Her breaths became short, her breathing labored. Panic overtook her. Was she losing her mind? Who put these words here? Who had sabotaged her work? Would she lose her job? Randy was right, she would probably face libel charges. These thoughts raced through her mind at breakneck speed. She couldn't think. She reached for the phone to call her father. *What am I doing?* Her hand went from the phone to her lap just as Jason came in. He was out of breath as if he'd been running. He closed the door and moved closer to her.

"Anne, Randy Vers tracked me down." He grasped her hand. "What is going on? You've never done anything like this."

Anne got up and wrapped her arms around him. Her breaths came in short, shallow bursts and she began to cry.

"I don't know what happened. I can't explain it." She sobbed into his jacket.

He stroked her hair. "Anne, darling, let's sit down and go through this." He withdrew a handkerchief from his pocket and handed it to her before helping her into her chair. He sat next to her.

"Randy says the transcript states that Sherman admitted hiding the money and that his wife will never find it." He paused to gather his next words. "Anne, he also tells me this is not what happened. In his testimony, Mr. Sherman denies this allegation." He waited for Anne to respond.

"Jason, I know. I was there. Sherman denied having hidden funds. I know what I heard. And I know what I wrote. At least, I'm reasonably sure. What I don't know is how the false information ended up in the transcript. Heaven knows I have an active imagination and I thought about what Sherman probably did. I even laughed about it with Gerard. But never in a million years would I falsify testimony." Her words started running together. Her temples pulsated. She watched Jason shove the transcripts into her briefcase.

He spoke softly. "Randy cancelled your case this morning. Dave can take mine. Let's go to the Jury Room and talk about this over a cup of coffee."

Anne felt like a robot. She followed Jason out of the courthouse and across the street to the Jury Room. The favored gathering place for attorneys and courtroom staff, the Jury Room was fashioned after an old English pub with dark cherry walls and hushed lighting. It had a large mahogany wraparound bar that filled the front room. Jason steered Anne around the bar to a leather booth in the back room.

They sat down and ordered coffee. Anne looked over at Jason and took his hand.

"Thank you for being here. I feel better now. Calmer." She took a sip, savoring the coffee's bouquet before proceeding. "This may sound weird, but last night I dreamed that my father was talking to me."

Jason looked puzzled. "Oh? What does that have to do with the Sherman case?"

"My father was telling me that Sherman had lied. That he had hidden his money in an offshore account."

Jason looked confused. "C'mon, Anne, I think your imagination is working overtime."

"No. It was like a real conversation, Jason. Not like a dream. My dad insisted that we do something. I'm worried. Do you think I'm losing my mind?" She searched Jason's face for an answer.

Jason touched her cheek. "No. I don't think you're losing your mind. But what possible explanation is there for what you typed into the transcript?"

"I don't know. For the life of me, I can't reconcile what I heard with what's recorded."

"Anne, I hope you're not suggesting that someone else overtook your writing. That's hocus-pocus." His forehead creased.

She shook her head and looked down at her hands. "I can't explain it rationally. I do know that the thought came to me in my dream." Anne supported her head with both hands. "I don't know what to think. But I have to fix it if I want to keep my job. And I don't want Sherman suing me for libel."

The two of them sat sipping coffee, without speaking. He patted her hand. "We'll figure something out."

"Randy said I should shred the copies."

"Good idea. I'll help you. Since Randy said he was the only one to see the transcripts, we'll destroy them and tell Gerard that your machine malfunctioned. These things happen. No one will be the wiser." Anne nodded.

"Thank God I have you." She smiled, but without mirth. Was she having a nervous breakdown? What was real? What was a dream? She wasn't sure she knew the difference.

"Let's get back to the office and make sure Randy covered all bases. I'll shred these." Anne nodded.

Back at the courthouse, Jason walked her to the elevator. "Since you don't have class today, let's grab an early dinner and try to relax." Anne felt grateful for his kindness and efforts to take her mind off the problem. She leaned over and pecked him on the cheek.

"Perfect. Just what I need. A quiet evening with you. Thanks."

5

Anne was relieved to find that Randy had covered her backside in court. Jason had shredded the transcripts, and Sherman versus Sherman had been rescheduled for the next morning. The rest of the day passed as though nothing unusual had happened. At seven she walked to the little Italian bistro near her apartment. She felt in control again. Centered.

Luigi's beckoned with its aromas of southern Italian cooking, checkered tablecloths, and arias by Luciano Pavarotti and other opera greats. Luigi greeted her with a kiss on each cheek and took her to a corner booth where Jason waited.

"Anna. It's always a pleasure to see you and Jason." Luigi said in his thick Neapolitan accent before leaving.

Jason got up and gave her a soft kiss. "Just what the doctor ordered," he assured her.

"You are so right."

They ordered a bottle of Chianti and the house special, a shrimp linguine with Alfredo sauce, then fell into easy conversation. The wine worked its magic and Anne relaxed. Since they had agreed this evening was for the two of them, she would not mention the transcript. Anne felt grateful for Jason's support–and love. By the time they left, she felt she was viewing the day's events in perspective. Jason walked her the two blocks to her apartment.

"You know, we should do this more often," she teased as they arrived at her door. *God it feels good to laugh.*

"You're right. And we shall." He pulled her to him, and covered her mouth with a hard kiss.

She returned his kiss with equal passion. Her body warmed.

"Are you sure you're okay? I can spend the night if you like," Jason asked as he pulled away.

"I'd love to spend the night with you, but I'm whipped. I need a good night's sleep so I'll be back to my old self by morning."

He took her face in his hands and gave her a tender kiss. "You know I love you."

"I love you too. I'll be fine."

Safely in her apartment, she watched Jason walk to his car. Anne hoped he wasn't worried. She knew her behavior must have appeared strange. She had tried to give an appearance of calmness, but Jason knew her better than anyone. Did she think she could fool him? Her thoughts returned to the transcript. She no longer doubted herself. She could not have made a mistake. There had to be an explanation. Did someone sabotage her work? Would Tim Sherman's attorneys stoop so low, hoping for a mistrial? Maybe. She racked her brain, but nothing fit. She would make some discrete inquiries tomorrow.

Anne turned away from the window and looked around. She had the sense that something was different. While nothing looked out of order, she couldn't dismiss the feeling. And she detected a faint smell of pipe tobacco–her father's tobacco. Memories of her father, coupled with the events of the day, overwhelmed her. Her eyes welled up.

Not now. I must stay calm and cool. It dawned on her that the tobacco smell must be coming from her new next-door neighbor. She had met him as he was moving in last month. He was a nice looking man in his mid-sixties. His wife had died the year before and he said he was "downsizing." From his many boxes of books, she assumed he was a professor. And he was probably a pipe smoker. She imagined him sitting in his wingback chair, sporting a corduroy jacket with patched elbows, pipe in hand, a glass of red wine, and a vintage copy of Chaucer. *Of course.* She told herself. That explained it.

She grabbed a soft drink on her way to the bedroom. After changing into her comfy sweats, she headed to the living room to watch some television. She heard the can hit the floor, spilling sticky soda over the hardwood. She wanted to scream, but nothing came out. Her heart threatened to break out of her chest. There was a man sitting in the wingback chair.

She dug her nails into the doorframe to steady herself. She felt her knees buckle and clung tighter to remain upright. Her chest tightened as she struggled to breathe. The man was staring at her. Was that her father? It couldn't be. Her father was dead. She felt confusion and terror. Who was he? How did he get in? What were his intentions?

She glanced at the front door and gauged the distance to it. Could she beat him to the door and get out? She had to try. Get to the door before he did. She inched a few feet toward it. He didn't budge. Whoever he was, he was not making a move. He just sat there, casually smoking his pipe. She watched the smoke rise from the bowl and form a ring above his head. It all seemed to be happening in slow motion, surreal, like a page from Kafka.

I've got to make it to the door. She was about to dive for it when the man took the pipe from his mouth and, in a familiar voice, said "Hello, Angel."

With that, Anne's legs gave out and she collapsed. *This can't be happening.* She opened one eye. He was still there, pipe in hand, smiling at her. It was her father who had called her "Angel." *But her father was dead.* This time her imagination had gone too far. Or she'd had a complete mental breakdown.

"Angel, it's me," he continued. "No reason to have such a dramatic reaction. It's your father. Talk to me."

Anne opened the other eye. *I've hit rock bottom. Now I'm talking to a ghost.* "I have gone completely bonkers," she mumbled to herself while pulling herself up. She stumbled to her couch, never averting her eyes from the man–or apparition–who claimed to be her father. "This is not real. I'm dreaming. I'm going to wake up now." She shook her head, blinked her eyes several times. He was still there.

"Angel, stop this nonsense," he said. "I am not a hallucination. I am real . . . well, at least as real as a ghost can be. But let's get down to business. First, how are you?"

"Oh great, now he wants to chat," Anne whispered.

"Okay, we won't 'chat'. Only I am a little hurt that you don't want to talk with your old dad after all this time. Never mind. I guess I can see that you are in shock."

"Shock?" Anne rebounded and felt her temper rising. "Shock? I'll say."

Before he could catch his next breath, if a ghost has a breath to catch, Anne continued.

"Why are you here and what do you want?"

"Now, Angel, is that any way to talk to your father?"

"Yes, exactly the way to talk to my deceased father who is sitting in my living room wanting to know how I have been." She couldn't recall ever having felt this angry.

She was bursting with questions. "I haven't been able to get a night's sleep because of dreams of you. Troubling dreams of you going on and on about the Shermans. You know anything about that?"

"I'm sorry but I was trying every way I knew to get your attention. I feel very strongly about what Tim is trying to do to dear Isabelle, and someone has to stop him."

"Wait a minute," Anne interrupted, "by someone, you can't possibly mean *me*?"

"Of course I do. Well, I really mean us. Who else can I count on? I can't do this on my own. Ghosts do have limited abilities you know. "

"No, I don't know. I haven't had much experience in teaming up with a ghost."

"Now, Anne Angel, let's not argue. I'm asking you to help me stop Tim before he succeeds. We always worked well together. What do you say?"

Anne remembered their good times and close relationship. For some crazy reason, she found herself softening. If this was not a hallucination and really was her father, she had no choice but to help him. She didn't like what Mr. Sherman seemed to be pulling either. Why not team up with her father to prevent Sherman's success. It was only her father after all. While debating herself, her father broke in.

"I'm very sorry about rewriting your transcript."

"You did that?" Her temper rose. Good thoughts about her father began to dissolve.

"First thing, Angel, I am so sorry about the transcript. Please forgive me." Anne found her voice. She leaned forward, shaking her finger, ready to tear into him. His voice stopped her in mid-breath.

"Before you jump all over me, hear me out. I had good reason to do what I did."

Anne sighed in exasperated. "This ought to be good."

"As you know, I never could tolerate people who don't play fair," he began. "And Tim is a liar and a self-indulgent bully."

Anne had to agree with that.

Her father continued. "Tim and Isabelle were clients when he set up his company. He was a nothing when he married Isabelle. She gave him his start and helped him build their business. Now, the business is successful and he's bored with her. He has a mistress, you know."

He saw that Anne had been listening intently. He stopped his story for a moment. He loved her so much. They had been so close.

"You know, Anne, I looked forward to having you as a partner, discussing cases, sharing clients, and seeing you evolve into an experienced attorney."

Anne nodded.

"Damn," he said. "Why did I have to have that heart attack?"

Anne stepped in, drawing him back to Tim Sherman.

"So, you rewrote my transcript? But why? And how?" Her wheels were spinning. She began to pace.

"Anne, Angel, I rewrote your transcript because that was the only way I could get your attention. I tried to reach you in your dreams. I tried to whisper in your ear in the courtroom."

"Ohmygod. That was you? During Mr. Sherman's testimony I had the feeling you were there." Tender feelings evaporated and morphed to anger once again. "But Dad, I could have lost my job. They could have sued me for libel. I would have been a laughing stock, been infested by locusts, and God knows what else because you screwed up my work. You of all people know how important transcripts are." She kept silent for a moment. "What in God's green acre were you thinking?" She turned and faced him square on.

"I guess I wasn't thinking. I took the chance. But, in my defense, I did arrange for Randy Vers to come in early and collect the transcripts." He chuckled. "Boy, that was not an easy maneuver."

Anne nodded, "I would bet not." She was running out of steam. Her eyes filled with tears, equal parts anger, frustration, and the realization that this might actually be her father.

"Anne, we have to get proof of Tim's offshore account to Randy as Isabelle's attorney. We can't let this jerk succeed. I'm not sure yet how to accomplish it. Together we'll figure it out." He put his pipe back in his mouth and started puffing.

"So that's it? Just get proof and all is right with the world?" It hit her that she was conversing with her dead father. If that wasn't bizarre enough, the two of them were plotting against a defendant in Judge Johnston's courtroom.

"Dad, this is too much for me to absorb right now. I don't want to find where Mr. Sherman is hiding his money and I don't want to continue this ridiculous conversation." She stomped her foot and turned toward her bedroom.

"I understand, Anne. This may be a little over the top right now."

"A little?" Anne turned to face him. "This is more than a little over the top. I'm going to my room now. And I'm going to sleep. It could be a sound sleep since you are here and not disturbing my rest or showing up in my dreams!" With that she turned and marched straight to the pantry. She pushed aside the rice cakes and grabbed the bag of Oreo cookies. This was certainly an emergency. She stomped into her bedroom, and slammed the door behind her. *Tomorrow. Tomorrow, tomorrow, tomorrow.*

"That's all right, Angel," he called through the closed door. "We'll talk in the morning."

"And don't mess with my work again," Anne hollered. With that she switched on the television, turning the volume higher than usual. She considered the matter closed.

Anne's father wished he could reassure her. He watched as she sat on her bed, glaring at the television. Her arms were firmly crossed and her lips were tightly pursed. He had seen that look so many times before. He was reminded when she was eight and had wanted to go to the mall on her own. She argued that it was not far, and she had memorized the streets. Of course, he had said no, and, of course, she responded in the same way–stomping off, arms crossed, lips pursed. Oh he was very familiar with her moods. He also knew she was a dear sweet person who would do anything to help another human being. Yes, she would come around.

•••••••

Tim Sherman was worried. Why had Isabelle's attorney requested a delay? Everything was going so well for him. Had they discovered something? He knew Stephanie was under control, and his attorneys had told him it was nothing to be concerned about. Judge Johnston told them it had something to do with correcting the transcripts. Tim accepted their assurances, but his gut told him otherwise.

For the first time since she had been hired, Anne called in sick. She hated lying, but there was no way she could put in a day's work. She assuaged her guilt with the thought that Judge Johnston would be able to find another court reporter.

Sipping a cup of coffee at her kitchen table, she filtered the myriad thoughts running through her head. Things seem so different in the morning. Had she conversed with her father last night? Of course not. People don't chat with ghosts. At least not normal, well-adjusted court reporters. In the light of morning, it all seemed so ridiculous. It must have been her imagination working overtime. Or maybe she'd drunk too much wine. There was no denying that her transcript had been rewritten. How could she explain that? Against her better judgment, she decided to investigate Tim Sherman a little further. She showered quickly, pulled on a pair of jeans and a lightweight sweater, and slipped into her Docksiders. Anne enjoyed a close relationship with her mother, so in crisis, home was the logical place to go.

She reached for the phone and dialed. Her mother, as usual, sounded pleased to hear Anne's voice. "Um, mom, I'd like to stop by. How about eleven or so?"

"Is something wrong?" Anne heard concern in her mother's voice. She wondered why she bothered pretending that all was hunky-dory. "Don't you have to work today?"

"Things are quiet, so I took the day off."

"Of course. I would love to see you. I'll put a fresh pot of coffee on."

"Great. See you soon." Anne hung up, grabbed her purse and rummaged through the clutter before finding her car keys under a pack of tissues. She was an organized person in most things, except for car keys. "This is why I take the bus," she said to herself.

On a whim she swung by the bakery and picked up a coffeecake. Nothing equips you to handle a crisis better than your Mother–and pastries.

She pulled up to her parents' house. Her mother stopped watering her flowerbeds. A statuesque woman with striking gray chin-length hair that framed her oval face, Sarah Marshall had an air of elegance that Anne wished she possessed. She smiled and waved, motioning Anne into the house.

Large pansy-filled flowerpots and sage green wicker furniture with flowered chintz pillows lined the front porch that ran the length of the mission-style house.

Anne grabbed the coffeecake from the front seat and met up with her mother. The two women embraced and walked side by side up the front steps.

"Coffee's ready. How did you know I was in the mood for some scrumptious coffeecake?" Mrs. Marshall took the cake from Anne and kissed her on the cheek. She looked concerned.

The kitchen was painted a sunny yellow. White café curtains hung at the windows and a fresh bouquet of daisies rested in a crystal vase on the counter. Her parents' house had been a gathering place for friends and neighbors as long as she could remember. Anne sat down and gazed out the French doors at the potted flowers on the patio. Her mother sliced the cake and poured the steaming liquid into oversized mugs. Anne inhaled the comforting aroma. Her mother sat down across from Anne and reached for her hand.

"Anne dear, what's wrong? Don't tell me nothing. A mother knows when things aren't right."

Anne took a few deep breaths. She knew better than to try and hide something from her mother. Over the years, their relationship had evolved from parent and child to friends.

She swallowed hard and told her mother about the rewritten transcript, the dreams of her father, and what she knew of the Shermans.

"I understand why you'd be upset. But there must be an explanation for the transcript. Is someone at the courthouse envious of you, or after your job?"

"No, Mom. That's not it. And that's not all. Dad spoke to me last night."

"I know. You said you dreamed about him."

"No, Mom. Not dreamed about Dad. He actually talked to me just like you and I are talking. He was sitting in my living room smoking his pipe."

"Anne dear, are you sure you just weren't hallucinating? The stress with the transcripts—"

"That's what I thought at first, but let me assure you, I had a full conversation with Dad. He is upset about Tim Sherman's attempts to swindle Isabelle."

"Now you are being silly. Why on earth would your Dad visit you in your living room and have any interest whatsoever in Tim and Isabelle Sherman?"

"That was my first reaction." Anne heard her voice rising and becoming more agitated. "But you know Dad. He never could stand an injustice. He wants my help in stopping Mr. Sherman." She saw the disbelief in her mother's face.

"Anne, I don't know what to say. This is a lot to take in."

Anne slumped into her chair and took a sip of her coffee. "Well, do you think I'm crazy?"

Her mother took time before answering.

"Of course not, dear. I wish I had a clue. But I have no idea." Mrs. Marshall stood and walked to the French doors. She opened them and the scent of lilacs filled the kitchen. She turned to face Anne. "I will tell you this much, Anne, I believe wholeheartedly that it is possible for the spirit of someone deceased to communicate with the living. It may be through dreams, automatic writing, or materializations. Yes, dear, I believe it is possible. I know you and your father had a strong connection—" Her voice trailed off.

Anne shifted in her chair. Her mother's acceptance comforted her. But she was not comfortable with the idea of communicating with the other side. And she was not convinced that it was true.

Her mother continued, in a soft and deliberate voice, "What I still do not understand is why he would be so involved with the Sherman case. When someone's spirit communicates with loved ones, I thought it was for a spiritual reason. Getting involved in a divorce proceeding doesn't make sense. It's a puzzler. And yet, it would be so typical of your father." She laughed, "He certainly loved a challenge. Especially to stop an injustice."

Anne considered what her mother had said. "Mom, has he ever come to you?"

"Oh, good heavens no," she responded without

hesitation. "He knows I would freak out." Mother and daughter chuckled. "I do feel his presence at times." She wore a thoughtful expression, as if remembering some special moments. "I think that piercing the veil between the spiritual and real world is a very special ability. I don't have it, but it appears that you do."

"I'm so grateful that you're accepting of this. Assuming that I have the gift, or ability, I wonder why is he so concerned about the Shermans?"

"I have no clue. We've known them for over twenty years. I always liked Isabelle. But I never cared much for Tim. He was never particularly likeable. He grew more self-absorbed as he became more successful."

"Dad said Mr. Sherman had a mistress who probably caused the rift between them. Do you know about that?"

Her mother took another sip. "There were rumors. You know how they gossip at the club. Everyone thought it was his office manager, Stephanie Burke. Of course I saw nothing to support it. And Isabelle never mentioned it. She's too much of a lady." Mrs. Marshall shrugged. "And who knows if Isabelle was even aware of this other woman."

Anne sat quietly, considering the information.

"Anne, if your father is truly manifesting himself to you, and he is determined to stop Tim from succeeding, what are you going to do?"

Anne shook her head and sighed. "I have no idea. I'd better go. I have work to do."

Anne kissed her Mother good-bye and drove to the law library.

•••••••

Anne found it difficult to focus on reviewing Evidence cases and her mind wandered. What if Tim Sherman was conspiring with his office manager to hide his assets from his wife? Her Dad had said the money was hidden in an offshore account. She wondered what to do next. As if on cue, she looked up and spotted Bryan Knightly from her study group. She waved him over.

"Hey, early bird. What are you doing here in the middle of the afternoon? Don't you have a job? And what happened to your pencil? Don't tell me you are back to that again."

She looked down at the skeletal remains of her pencil. *Darn. I hope I don't get wood poisoning.* "I have some time off, so where else would I spend it."

"Of course."

Anne took the opportunity to pick Bryan's brain.

"Bryan, hypothetically speaking, how would one set up an offshore account?" The way he moved closer and locked her in his gaze, she knew she'd piqued his interest.

"Hypothetically?"

Anne kept silent.

Bryan continued. "I'll go along because knowing you, I probably don't want to know."

Anne maintained her silence. He continued. "Setting up an offshore account is relatively easy. You can do it in person or via mail. Switzerland, Luxembourg, Singapore, and the Cayman Islands are the most popular places. There are differences, depending on your purpose. In Switzerland, the key feature is secrecy and in most matters, like divorce, the information is considered private."

Anne's ears perked up. Then she considered. Sherman didn't appear to be sophisticated enough for Switzerland.

Bryan continued, "Luxembourg and Singapore are favored for investment opportunities and tax breaks. The Cayman Islands are different." Anne leaned forward. "The Caymans are geared to corporations. If someone wants secrecy above all else, this is the way to go. Am I boring you?"

"Absolutely not, I want to know more, especially about the Caymans."

"Offshore accounts are usually suspect. Many of them are for illegal purposes, like hiding money so it won't be taxable–or hiding assets from an ex-wife. In the Caymans, it's possible to open an account in the name of a corporation. That becomes the only name the bank knows. There's no need for a person to reveal his identity. So he doesn't risk the effects of disclosure. If you're really clever, you can create a series of corporations leaving a paper trail that never leads back to you." Bryan paused. "Too much information? And why do you want to know? Oops, I forgot. I don't want to know."

"Thank you, Bryan. You've given me everything I need for the moment. Now on to Evidence cases." They opened their casebooks, spreading papers all over the table. Anne mulled over this new information. As she did, Maria, Clark, and John showed up to complete the study group.

Because Anne liked Evidence class, it flew by. Before she knew it, she was home and looking forward to the weekend and no classes until

Monday. She turned the lock on her door, sniffed for signs of her father, and found none. She sighed in relief. But the intrigue still piqued her interest. *A chip off the old block.*

She grabbed a bag of chips and a soda and settled down for some mindless television. It was only ten o'clock so she knew Jason would still be up. She had been avoiding his calls all day. The time had come to face his questions. He picked up on the first ring.

"I have been trying to get hold of you all day. Are you all right? I was worried sick." He sounded close to hysteria. "First they tell me you called in sick, then you don't return my calls. I must have tried a dozen times to reach you. Anne, what's going on?"

"Jason, darling, I'm sorry that you're upset. I'm perfectly fine. The events of the last few days affected me more profoundly than I realized. I am terribly upset by the Sherman case so I took a sick day. I took a coffeecake to my mother and spent the afternoon studying."

"Is there anything I can do? Do you want me to come over?"

"No. I am feeling much better. I just needed a day by myself. I'm so sorry for not returning your calls. But we're talking now."

The concern left his voice. "How is your mother?"

"She is fine. The visit was great therapy. So how did Judge Johnston survive without me? Did the Sherman trial continue? Who covered for me?"

"Yes, the Judge somehow survived without you," he joked, "and the trial went on. However, Randy Vers told me that you missed all the excitement. Tim Sherman's office manager, Stephanie Burke, was in the courtroom and it created quite a stir. The defense was going to call her to testify. They were counting on her to verify that nothing out of the ordinary was going on. But she never testified." Anne sat up.

"What happened?"

"You wouldn't believe it. When Mrs. Sherman saw Stephanie in the courtroom, she went crazy, started screaming at her. Calling her all kinds of names–none of which included 'office manager.' You should have been there."

"Tell me everything."

"Well, the gossip is that Stephanie Burke is Tim Sherman's mistress and the reason for the divorce. The courtroom became so disruptive that Judge Johnston called for a recess until Monday morning."

Anne was spellbound. What her mother and

father had told her must be true. This meant there might be some validity to the accusation that Sherman had hidden his assets. She sure picked the wrong day to call in sick and miss all the excitement.

She hesitated and chose her words carefully. "Was there any mention of offshore accounts?"

"Anne, you probably shouldn't mention this to anyone else. You barely escaped a libel suit with the transcript. It was only dumb luck that—"

"I know, I know!" She felt agitated and couldn't hide the irritation in her voice. She softened her tone. "I'm sorry, Jason. I know you're right."

"It's okay. Let's grab dinner and a movie tomorrow night."

"Sounds wonderful. Let's touch base in the afternoon." They said their good nights. Anne slept peacefully that night with no unsolicited visitors from the other side.

•••••••

Bryan threw his briefcase on the kitchen table.

"Hey watch it," Celia Knightly cautioned and grabbed her mug to keep it from spilling.

"Sorry. Glad to be home. It was a long day." He

leaned over and gave her a kiss.

"How are the kids? Any bank robberies or kidnapped neighbors I need to know about?"

Celia shook her head, "Not that the cops have reported yet, so I think we're safe."

"In that case, life is good." He poured himself a cup of coffee and joined her at the table. "I had the strangest conversation with Anne Marshall at school tonight. She wanted to know everything about offshore accounts. What do you think that was all about?"

"Beats me. Some paper she is working on?"

"No. We're in the same classes. I would know that. It's something more. She claims its innocent curiosity, but Anne is up to something."

Celia turned to the Local News in the newspaper she was reading and slid it over to Bryan. "Think it has anything to do with the divorce case between Isabelle and Tim Sherman? According to the story, Isabelle is accusing Tim of hiding money."

"In an offshore account," Bryan finished her sentence. "Of course. Anne is a court recorder and I'll bet she is on that case." He was feeling pleased with himself. "She should know better than to try and fool me," he laughed. "They don't call me eagle-eye for no reason."

"Oh, now you have a nickname?" Celia questioned.

"Well, not actually, but you know what I mean. Why would you know about this case anyway?"

"You know Tommy, Simon's friend? His mother, Alice, works for Tim Sherman."

"You're kidding." Bryan was suddenly interested. "What does she do there?"

"She's one of the office workers. She files and does clerical work for him. She really dislikes him. She said he made a pass at her once. Can you imagine that? A happily married mother of three and this slime bag makes a move on her."

"Why didn't she quit or turn him in for sexual harassment?"

"She needs the job. They are buying a house and need the money."

"That sucks." Bryan affirmed. Then he got an idea. "Do you think she has any information on his clients or activities?"

"I don't know. What kind of information?" Celia was cautious.

"Client lists, financial statements, things like that."

"I'm seeing her after school tomorrow. I'll ask. She would love to burn that guy."

Bryan felt a surge of excitement. If he could look over client lists or any financial information, he might be able to find something he could share with Anne. From what Celia said, this guy deserved to be caught.

•••••••

Tim Sherman had a horrible night. He tossed and turned. He felt he was losing control. That day in the courtroom had been a disaster. He had rehearsed Stephanie in preparation for her testimony. She would corroborate his testimony that there was nothing abnormal with his company's finances. With no proof otherwise, case closed. He'd be granted a divorce; he'd tie up loose ends, and leave. He was certain that his wife Isabelle's attorneys had told her that Stephanie would be testifying. He had been foolish to believe Isabelle would remain calm. He didn't understand women—or care to. He just wanted this over. After the scene in the courtroom, Stephanie had become hysterical. He pulled out all the stops to calm her. And he agreed to spend the night with her in the hope of reassuring her that everything would be all right. He rolled over and saw that Stephanie was asleep. *Easy for her. She doesn't have everything to lose.* He wondered what Isabelle was up to. He'd seen a different side of her that disquieted him, and he spent the rest of the night staring at the ceiling.

•••••••

Randy Vers bolted awake. What was he dreaming about? Jim Marshall? *My God, Jim's been dead for over two years.* Randy got out of bed and went to the bathroom for a glass of water. His frustration with the Sherman case flooded over him like a bad dream. He couldn't explain it, but the case haunted him. He knew in his gut Tim Sherman was cheating Isabelle but had nothing to substantiate his suspicion. Then, Anne Marshall puts his suspicions into the transcript as if Tim Sherman had actually confessed. *Why would she do that?* This case was falling apart. If he hadn't been compelled to go in early and retrieve the transcripts, God knows what would have happened. Mistrial? Now, on top of everything, he was having nightmares about Jim, his old friend and mentor. He sat on the side of the bed.

"Can't sleep?" Ilene asked.

"No. This Sherman case is driving me crazy."

"Still can't find where he's hiding his money?"

"It's not only that. Anne Marshall put in the transcript that Sherman admitted having an offshore account."

"Did he say that?"

"No. He adamantly denied it."

"That's strange for Anne." Ilene was puzzled.

"I know. Luckily, I caught it before Tim Sherman's attorneys did and we were able to correct it."

"Lucky for Anne too."

Randy nodded. "I can't figure out how or why she did that."

"Why don't you ask her?"

"Good ole' female logic. You know, I think I will." Ilene smiled.

"There's something else." Randy hesitated. "I've been having nightmares about Jim Marshall."

Ilene put her arms around his shoulders. "You miss him don't you?"

"More than I realized." He kissed her hand and lay back on his pillow.

Ilene rolled toward Randy and gave him a soft loving kiss. "Since we're both awake—"

• • • • • • •

Anne finished work by noon so she grabbed a salad, which she nibbled at on the way to the law library. She'd have plenty of time to study before Jason picked her up at seven.

She hunkered down at the library and lost herself in property law. When someone tapped her shoulder, she jumped. Expecting to see a fellow classmate, she turned and saw Randy Vers standing over her.

"Hi, Anne." His eyes darted about and he looked uncomfortable.

"Randy, if this is about that mix-up with the transcript, I am so sorry. I know Jason shredded all copies and you covered with the judge. Is something wrong?"

"No, no. That's all behind us." He sat down across from her. "Is there someplace we can talk privately?" He pleaded, "I need your help."

"Of course. Let's go down to the lunchroom." She closed her books and tucked her study pages into her briefcase.

They took a table in the corner. "What's this all about, Randy?"

He looked around before speaking. Anne had to strain to hear him. "I admit that I was shocked by the transcript and the allegations of an offshore account. Now I can't shake this nagging voice in my head that tells me there may be something to it."

Anne remained silent.

"Anne, do you think there could be something to this?"

She believed there was. She also knew that her father would stop at nothing until this was settled. "I'm not sure. Tell me, how can I help?"

Randy took a breath and sat back in his chair. "If Sherman has hidden assets in an offshore account, how did you know about it?"

Anne cut him off. "I didn't know about it. I know how it looks, but I swear I have no idea how that appeared in the transcription. I'm as upset as you are."

He changed his line of questioning. "Let's say, for argument's sake, that there are funds in an offshore account. Any ideas about finding them?"

Anne shared with Randy what Bryan had told her.

"Does Bryan have any ideas? God knows, I don't."

"I didn't ask."

Randy looked down at his hands and sighed.

It was an awkward moment. Anne jumped in.

"I heard I missed quite a scene in the courtroom today. Sorry I wasn't there."

Randy perked up. "You heard about that, huh? Isabelle took offense at Stephanie Burke being in the courtroom."

"From what I hear, it was pandemonium."

Randy laughed. "A bit."

"You know, rumor has it Tim Sherman is having an affair with Stephanie. I think she knows something about the offshore account. It's just a hunch, but I believe if you break Stephanie, you'll find the account."

Randy nodded. Anne couldn't read his expression. "You have a lot of studying to do, so I'll let you go. I can't thank you enough for talking to me." He smiled as he stood and turned to leave, then turned around. "You know, I'm been thinking a lot about your Dad lately."

Anne shot up in her seat. "Really?" *Calm down.*

"Yeah. Isn't that strange?" He shook his head then leaned over and whispered, "Let's keep this conversation to ourselves. Don't want to tip anyone off."

"My lips are sealed." She watched him leave. *Where to go from here?* She looked forward to her father's guidance.

•••••••

Jason arrived promptly at seven. Anne was famished and looking forward to a nice evening out. They had agreed on *Casino Royale*, the latest James Bond movie. She fought the impulse to tell Jason about her conversation with Randy. The men were too close to risk betraying Randy and losing his trust. Maybe she'd vent to Maria. Maria had no reason to tell anyone, so it was safe. *What good is a secret if you can't share it?* According to Anne's rule for secrets, it was okay to share with someone who doesn't know the players. She doubted that Randy expected her to keep silent.

Anne felt grateful that Jason asked nothing about the Shermans, offshore accounts, or her father. As Jason walked Anne back to her apartment, he put his arm around her waist. It felt good to be close to him. At her door he kissed her with a passion that made her toes warm.

"Do you want to stay?" she whispered in his ear.

"Absolutely." He swept her up in his arms. He carried her over the threshold and directly into the bedroom, where he gently placed her on her bed. He lay down beside her and covered her with kisses while running his hand the length of her body. Anne responded with all the eagerness of a hungry lioness. It had been much too long since they'd made love.

She woke Saturday morning to the smell of coffee brewing. She reached over to feel Jason's side of the bed, which was empty. She slipped into a terry robe and slippers and padded toward the kitchen. Jason sat reading the New York Times and half listening to the morning news on the television. He looked up and smiled.

"I have coffee ready for you."

"You are an absolute angel."

They spent the rest of the morning relaxing and reading the paper. Anne liked to work the crossword and Jason buried himself in the sports section. Hearing a soft meowing outside her door, Anne got up to let in Aristotle. He ignored her and jumped onto Jason's lap.

"Aristotle, you are the most fickle cat I know," Anne admonished. Aristotle just snuggled closer to Jason, who was rubbing the cat's ears. Aristotle's loud purr told her the feline was in cat heaven.

"Have fun studying." Jason teased as he readied to leave around noon.

"I love you. I'll call you when I get home."

He kissed her. "Love you too." He hesitated for a moment, stroking her hair. "You seem to be your old self again. I'm relieved."

•••••••

There was no sign of Maria when Anne reached the law library. She pulled out her cell phone and called Maria's house. Shane, Maria's husband, answered.

"Hi, Anne. Maria's on her way. She should be there any minute now."

"Thanks, Shane. Enjoy your day of peace and quiet."

"Since I'm in homicide, I doubt that will happen," he reminded her, "but thanks for the good thought. Hey, when are you and Jason coming over for pizza and another game of Trivial Pursuit? We are still the reigning champions."

"Don't taunt me. You know it's only temporary, so don't get comfortable." Anne spotted Maria. "Maria's here. I'll check with Jason and let you know about getting together."

Anne waved Maria to the table and filled her in on everything that had happened with the Sherman case, except the part about her father.

"Anne, I'm troubled that you've made Isabelle Sherman's attorney a co-conspirator. As an officer of the court, you shouldn't be giving information to one of the parties in a lawsuit, especially when you are involved."

"You're right, Maria. But, technically it wasn't information—just hunches."

Maria raised her eyebrows.

Anne continued. "I'm having trouble figuring out how to get Stephanie Burke to spill the beans."

"You know how it goes in homicide interrogations, we tell one of the bad guys he's been betrayed by his partner. And it usually works. And no one talks faster than a betrayed mistress." Anne digested Maria's words as her friend continued. "What Mrs. Sherman's attorney has to do is convince Stephanie that Sherman was using her and had no intention of running off with her. Who knows, he may even have another girlfriend. Or maybe he wants to reconcile with his wife. In any case, someone has to convince Stephanie that she will never see a dime of the money she helped hide." Maria snapped her fingers. "Piece of cake. It works every time."

Anne wondered how Randy could pull it off.

That was the million-dollar question. Soon Bryan, John, and Clark joined them, so Anne stopped talking about the Sherman case. She couldn't wait to get home and call Randy.

At six, Maria declared their "quality study time" was at an end and she had a husband to tend to. They packed up their books. Bryan took Anne aside and asked if she needed any more information on offshore accounts. Anne assured him that she had all she needed. Bryan gave her a look that said *I know you are not telling me everything, but I can wait.* They walked together in silence to their cars.

•••••••

Maria entered her apartment and immediately felt her shoulders relax. *A nice quiet evening at home. No law school. No homicides.* "Hey Irish, I'm home," she called. From the mouth-watering aroma of Irish stew, she knew Shane had been busy. He appeared from the kitchen wearing his "Kiss the Cook" apron.

"Is that my saucy wife I hear?" He lifted her off her feet and swung her around.

"It is, and the stew smells scrumptious. How

did you know I was hungry for stew?"

"My intuition, my dear. Have a glass of wine while I finish up. I'll call you when it's ready."

"Sounds wonderful." Maria poured herself a glass of wine, put in a Frank Sinatra CD, and plopped in her comfy chair in the living room.

Maria came from a long line of cops. Her father had been a Captain in the Chicago Police Department. She remembered how handsome he looked in his uniform. From the time she was a small child, she would crawl up on his large lap and snuggle. For her sixteenth birthday, he rented the local Moose Hall and invited all her friends, the neighbors, and half of his squadron for a huge Latino Party. He was her first dance partner. She remembered the glass ball turning and the lights flickering around the room while the band played "Sixteen Candles." She had felt like a princess. The next day he was killed. Shot while leaving the courthouse for testifying against the defendant. Her world crashed around her and life was never the same. From that moment, there was no doubt she would follow in his footsteps, along with her three brothers. That's when she met Shane. Life had become bearable again.

"Soup's up," Shane called from the dining room.

Maria pulled herself from the chair and joined him at the table.

"How was study group?" Shane asked. "Anything interesting?"

"There was something curious. Anne is involved in the Sherman divorce case. You remember that big shot who is being accused of hiding his money from his soon to be ex-wife."

"Yeah. It's been in the papers."

"Anne is the court reporter. She asked me how to make his girlfriend turn on him."

"That should be easy ... jealousy," Shane laughed. "Works all the time."

"That's what I told her. She seemed really keen. I warned her not to step over the ethical line. In fact, she may have already done it."

"How so?"

"She was conspiring with Mrs. Sherman's attorney to get evidence against Mr. Sherman. I'm worried about how far she will go"

"Not good. You did the right thing to warn her. By the way, Anne said she and Jason would pick a night to come over for a Trivial Pursuit rematch."

"They know they're no match for this dynamic duo."

"You got that right." He ladled stew into Maria's

bowl.

Maria dipped her bread in the broth. "I knew there was a reason I married such a handsome Irishman."

· · · · · · ·

Anne entered her apartment. The smell of pipe tobacco greeted her.

Here we go again. She dropped her books on the kitchen table, grabbed a bottle of water and moved to the living room. "Okay, Dad, you can come out now," she taunted.

"What a tone from my number one daughter," her father replied.

"I'm your only daughter."

"True enough," he conceded. He sat in the wingback chair, smoking his pipe, as if he belonged there. What startled her was not his presence, but her growing ease and familiarity with the situation.

"I like the direction you're taking. But I think it is time we step it up a notch."

"And how, pray tell, would we do that?"

"As I see it, Stephanie Burke knows where the account is, the name on the account, the password, numbers and all the necessary information. The challenge is getting her to spill it." He paused to tap his pipe on an ashtray that didn't exist. "Your friend, Detective O'Malley, is right. A woman scorned doesn't hesitate to push her lover under a bus."

"I agree, but how do we get her to that point?"

"Jealousy, my dear. Jealousy. Show her that Tim has already taken up with a new piece of fluff–or at least suggest it. Make her believe she is on her way out."

Anne began to comment. He cut her off.

"To stir the pot, I believe Randy should hire a private detective. Tim is a womanizer and will never change. Time is of the essence. Pass that on to him when you call him tonight. By the way, his number is in the book." With that he disappeared.

She looked up Randy's number and dialed.

He answered on the first ring. "I was just thinking about you. I had the strangest feeling you were going to call."

Oh boy, another "feeling." Thanks, Dad. Anne conveyed the information she had collected, including her suspicion that Sherman already had a new girlfriend. "If you hire a private detective right away, you may find what you need. You must move quickly, Randy."

"I understand. We're scheduled for court Monday morning, but I think I can delay it—for a while at least. I'll call a private eye I know. Thanks Anne. See you Monday."

As she hung up, Anne wondered what she had gotten into.

Her next call was to Jason. She wanted to hear his voice and hoped he could bring her back to reality.

"Hey you," she began, "how was your day without the love of your life?"

"When you put it that way," he laughed, "lonely, yet productive. How was the law library? Learn anything useful?"

"I learned more about property law than I ever wanted to know, thank you very much," she retorted. "I can fill you in if you have a few hours."

"No, please spare me," he recoiled. "I would much rather talk about us and how fabulous you are. And how much I love you. Maybe I haven't told you that enough lately."

"I love you too," Anne whispered. She thought about their night of lovemaking and felt her body flush.

"You know the weekend isn't over yet."

"I'll be there in ten minutes." Anne hung up and grabbed her purse as she bolted out the door.

7

Anne woke to Jimmy Buffet. This was hardly Margaritaville, but she looked forward to getting back to work.

At the courthouse, Randy darted into the elevator behind Anne, barely making it before the doors closed.

They nodded to each other. "Oh, by the way, Anne," Randy said, "Mrs. Sherman is ill today and the trial has been continued for a day or two so she can recover." The elevator stopped and Randy walked down the hallway to the courtrooms.

Way to go, Randy. As Anne neared her office, Shirley Williams, the Court Administrator, accosted Anne. Sixtyish and professionally dressed in a navy suit, Shirley had been running the courthouse for decades. She had seen administrative judges come and go, and the courtrooms always ran smoothly under Shirley's watch. Recently widowed, she now spent most of her time traveling to see her grandchildren. Her office was plastered with their pictures and clay sculptures etched with "World's Best Grandmother."

"I just saw Mr. Vers," she began. "He tells me you may be free for the next few days. I need you in Courtroom A. Sally is out sick and they are starting a trial on a breach of contract case. I knew you would be willing to help me out.

"Okay," Anne said.

"Thanks, you're a dear. And by the way, I left a new box of pencils on your desk." Before Anne could answer, Shirley was halfway down the hall furiously jotting notes. Anne gathered her supplies and headed for Courtroom A.

•••••••

Tim Sherman received the news early Monday that the trial had been continued for a few days. Something about Isabelle being under the weather. *That woman is up to something.* He was so close and now things were falling apart. He had objected to a delay, but his attorneys said it was out of their hands. "What difference would a day or two make?"

they assured him. *A hell of a lot of difference!* Now Stephanie was coming unglued and he was worried about her next court appearance. He was weary of them all. In need of a diversion, he whipped out his client book and thumbed through the pages. He had made notes next to the names of attractive clients so he could remember their "assets." He paused at Gloria Hutchins. Ah, yes. A sexy redhead, about thirty, with breasts the size and firmness of ripe honeydews. He had handled the estate of her deceased elderly husband. They had exchanged knowing glances at each meeting. He had little doubt that she was his for the taking. He picked up the phone and dialed her number. Her voice was as deep and sensuous as he remembered. He felt certain that she was all his. Most women were. They agreed to meet for dinner. He made reservations at a secluded hotel outside of town. He started to salivate as he thought of this impending conquest.

•••••••

"Is that you, Bryan?" Celia called as she heard the garage door open.

"Present and accounted for. What's up?"

"Remember Tommy's mother, Alice? The one who works for Tim Sherman? She was able to get some information for you to look at." Celia pointed to a pile of papers on the kitchen counter.

Bryan lunged at the stack. "How did she get these?"

"She said it was easy. The papers were left in the file room on the table."

Bryan grabbed the stack and flipped through it. Client lists, financials, phone logs. "Celia, I don't think we should have this. I'm having second thoughts about involving us in this." He backed away from the counter. "I had to be insane to even suggest this."

"Nonsense. Tim Sherman is a scumbag. But if it makes you feel any better, Alice said everything was out in plain sight. They had been copied for the subpoena. Both attorneys already have this."

"Do you know that for sure?"

"That's what she said."

Bryan breathed easier. "In that case, let's have a look." He took the stack to his office and started methodically searching the records. He didn't know exactly what he was looking for, but he would know it when he saw it. He spent the next hour searching the information, then realized how tired he was. *That's enough for tonight.* He gathered the documents and put them in his file drawer. He had just drifted off when it struck him what was missing. *Of course.* He sat upright in bed. *I have to be sure.* Tomorrow he would call his friend Roger from his old accounting firm.

•••••••

The next several days flew as Anne covered several hearings. On Thursday, Isabelle Sherman was well enough to appear in court.

Anne felt energized to be back on the Sherman trial. She took her position in Judge Johnston's courtroom and fidgeted while awaiting the circus to reconvene. Gerard was busy signing entries and handing out documents to a bevy of attorneys. He looked up momentarily and Anne caught his eye. He nodded and smiled.

A commotion near the courtroom door drew Anne's attention. She turned to see the Shermans and their entourage of attorneys, press, and curious onlookers file in. Mrs. Sherman was elegantly dressed in a soft pink cashmere suit and triple strand of pearls. Randy held her right arm. He looked up and winked at Anne. The gesture made Anne uneasy and her stomach knotted. Tim Sherman sat down, his expression as arrogant as ever. The bailiff called the courtroom to order and Judge Johnston entered.

Randy had reserved the right to recall Sherman, who strutted up to the witness box as if he owned it. He shot Randy an intimidating look as he was seated. Anne recognized Randy's style: deliberate yet relaxed. She knew that Randy did it to give the witness a false sense of security, right before he tightened the noose.

Randy asked Sherman some general questions. By his air of bravado, it was apparent that Sherman felt in control. Anne glanced around the courtroom and saw Stephanie Burke slip in and take a seat in the last row. Isabelle Sherman seemed unaware of Stephanie's presence.

"Mr. Sherman," Randy began, "is it true that you are having an affair?" He asked the question in a conversational tone as he walked away from the witness box. Anne watched Sherman's neck tighten.

"Objection!" shouted Sherman's attorney. Randy explained the pertinence of his question and said he would soon demonstrate its relevance to the court. Judge Johnston allowed the line of questioning.

"Of course not." Sherman replied with a red face. Randy turned and looked in Stephanie's direction–lingering long enough to tip off his client. Anne could see that Stephanie was edgy. Isabelle Sherman turned and looked in Stephanie's direction and stood momentarily. One of her attorneys grabbed her arm and whispered something. Isabelle sat down and fixed her gaze on her estranged husband.

Randy continued, "Can you tell me, Mr. Sherman, about your relationship with Stephanie Burke?" The entire courtroom turned to look at Stephanie. A low murmur filled the room.

Sherman stiffened. In a defiant tone he said, "Ms. Burke is my office manager. Our relationship is purely professional."

Randy didn't lose a beat.

"Mr. Sherman, are there any other women in your life, other than your wife of course, that you are involved with personally?" Sherman wore a menacing look. Everyone turned to look at Stephanie who leaned forward to better hear what her lover would say.

"Absolutely no one but my wife," he answered, too loudly. He crossed his arms and looked at the ceiling.

"No more questions your honor." Sherman flashed a surprised look at the Judge. "You may step down, Mr. Sherman."

"I would now like to call Ms. Stephanie Burke." Randy announced. Stephanie rose. Shoulders back and head high, she strode up the aisle opposite Isabelle Sherman to the witness box.

Smart move. Anne thought.

Stephanie was sworn in and Randy asked a few innocuous questions to loosen her up. He walked over to the plaintiff's table, withdrew several photographs from a folder, and asked that they be entered into evidence. After objections from Mr. Sherman's attorneys, Judge Johnston allowed the photos. Randy showed them to Anne so she could mark them as exhibits. The photos were of Sherman and a gorgeous redhead—definitely not Stephanie—in a very compromising situation. *Wow. Her old dad was right on target.*

Randy took the photos to Stephanie and asked her to identify the people in the picture. She grabbed the photos from his hand, stared at the first one for a split second, and flipped through the rest. It only took a minute for it to register with her. She ripped the photos into pieces.

"You sonofabitch!" she screamed at Sherman. "You lying sack of shit. You told me that Gloria was just a client!" She looked again at what remained of the pictures in her hand. Before anyone could stop her, Stephanie leaped out of the witness box and charged the defense table. She lurched across the table and grabbed Sherman by the throat. Yanking his tie and screaming obscenities, she continued her tirade until courtroom security arrived. They grabbed her legs as she clawed at Sherman.

"You sonofabitch." It took four men to separate her from Sherman and haul her thrashing from the courtroom.

Tim sat motionless. He was rubbing his neck. Anne could see the red scratches down his throat. The courtroom was quiet as a church. Judge Johnston rapped his gavel and called a recess until the following morning. He reminded the attorneys that their witnesses were still under oath. Randy collected the photo scraps. Anne thought he looked smug. When the courtroom had emptied, he turned to Anne and gave her a wink.

Everything had been set in motion. The "pot had been stirred" as her father had suggested.

Now they simply had to wait.

Anne was eager to tell Jason and her study group about the day's excitement. She ran into Jason as she was leaving her office. He grabbed her hand and pulled her into an alcove near the elevators. Before Anne could say anything, he covered her mouth with a warm kiss. She reciprocated and pressed against him. They separated and peeked into the hallway to make sure the coast was clear.

"Wow, what was that all about?" she asked.

"Just a reminder of how much I love you. I knew I wouldn't see you tonight and I wanted to remind you."

"Well, I'm glad you felt the urge," she responded. "Did you hear about the outburst in the courtroom?"

"No. What happened?"

She filled him in, omitting the part about her tip to Randy. She was uncertain how Jason would react to her collaboration with her father's ghost.

"I can't wait to see Randy. And to think I thought this was going to be a dull day." He gave Anne's hand a squeeze and sauntered down the hall.

•••••••

Anne arrived at law school and went straight to the lunchroom where Bryan and Maria were reviewing evidence cases.

"Wait 'till I tell you what happened today." She could barely contain her excitement.

"Hold on," Maria interrupted. "Slow down. Is this about the hidden money in the divorce settlement you told me about last week?"

Bryan jumped in.

"Wait a minute? Hidden money in a divorce?"

Damn! Bryan was on to her.

"So this offshore bank account stuff was not hypothetical, which, by the way I knew it wasn't. In fact, I had the opportunity to review some of Tim Sherman's records and you're right."

Anne was shocked. "How did you know it was Tim Sherman and how did you get his records?"

Bryan fell silent.

"I'd like to hear this too," Maria chimed in.

"Come on Anne. It's in all the newspapers. I only had to put two and two together to know it was Tim Sherman."

"I'll give you that one. There is a lot of publicity."

"The papers that were part of the subpoena were easy to see. Public record and all." Bryan lied.

"I don't think—" Anne started.

"Whatever," Bryan interrupted. "I reviewed the documents and I know at least one piece that is missing. I'm waiting for confirmation. That is, if you want my help?"

Anne felt a surge of energy. If Bryan could find something, this would be what Randy needed. Her mind was racing.

"Hold it both of you," Maria cautioned. "I don't buy this crap about you having access to the information. I am not going to ask you how you got it, and I don't want to hear." She glared at both of them.

Anne and Bryan exchanged a look. That was all Maria needed.

"You are both on shaky ground and you better back off. Understand?"

Anne and Bryan shook their heads. "Okay. We agree," Anne promised.

Maria was not convinced. She knew Anne. She had now involved Bryan as well as Randy Vers. She needed to stay close to Anne, if nothing more than to keep her out of trouble.

"Anyway," Anne continued, "You are not going to believe what happened in court today. Randy Vers surprised Stephanie Burke with photos of

Tim Sherman with another woman. She went ballistic. Maybe now she will turn on Tim."

Maria leaned over and whispered, "Watch your step, Anne. Make sure you keep me posted."

"Will do."

On cue Clark and John came in and conversation about the Shermans stopped.

In the parking lot Bryan stopped Anne. "As soon as I get confirmation on my suspicion I'll let you know."

"Thanks Bryan. I appreciate your help."

On her way home, Anne looked forward to the familiar pipe smell. As she'd imagined, her dad was sitting in the wingback chair puffing away.

"How did class go, Angel?"

"The usual." She put her briefcase down and grabbed a bottle of water. She plopped down on the couch. "I assume you were in court today and saw everything?"

"I certainly was and I certainly did," he responded. "I knew it was only a matter of time before Tim would find another conquest. I just wasn't sure he was stupid enough, with everything at stake, to act on his desires. I'm pleased that Randy took our advice and acted quickly."

"Maria feels that Stephanie will turn on Tim now that she has been scorned."

"I concur," said her father. "Now we just wait and see."

"Something else happened. Bryan helped himself to Tim Sherman's records and may have uncovered something to help Randy."

They shared a moment of silence. Anne looked at her dad and was flooded with memories. She loved him so much and missed him more than she realized. She remembered when she had run into the neighbor's hedge with her new two-wheeled bicycle. He had tended to her scrapes and then insisted the best way to recuperate was with a large banana split. She could almost taste the whipped cream.

"I know, Anne," he said softly. "I know."

Anne nodded her head. She reluctantly pushed herself up from the couch. "I'm exhausted. I'm going to bed." Her dad's pipe smoke hung in the air as Anne snuggled under the covers and fell asleep.

•••••••

Tim Sherman couldn't image that things could be any worse. How had things gotten so out of control? Stephanie was furious, acting like a maniac. She was threatening to tell his wife everything–the affair, the offshore account–everything. He had called Stephanie repeatedly, just to get her voice mail. Knowing that she always read her e-mails, Sherman tried that tact to get her attention. She was easy to manipulate, but he needed to see her in person. He chose his words carefully. Gloria had seduced him. It was not his fault. He blamed Isabelle for setting him up. His fat fingers pecked away.

Stephanie, darling. How can you doubt my love for you? You are the only one in my life. Let's get this over so we can be married and spend the rest of our lives together. Please, just talk to me. This is all Isabelle's fault. I love you more than life itself. Meet me at our favorite restaurant tonight and let me beg for your forgiveness. I love only you.

Always. Tim

While he waited for her reply, Sherman tried calling several more times. No answer. He felt desperate. There was no way this bimbo was going to destroy his plan. He checked his incoming messages again. His heart raced when he saw a message from Stephanie. Yes! She agreed to meet him. He sighed in relief. One way or another he would get Stephanie back under control.

8

Anne strode into the courtroom early, pumped up and primed. She couldn't wait to hear Stephanie's testimony. *This should be good. Any woman worth her salt would throw this guy under the bus.* She scanned the courtroom for the star witness. No Stephanie. Where could she be? In the restroom putting on fresh war paint? She watched Randy approach Gerard. Together they went into the judge's chambers. *What's that about?* A few minutes later, the door opened and Randy walked over to Anne. He was agitated.

"Randy—" She was anxious to tell him about the information Bryan was working on but he interrupted her.

"Stephanie is nowhere to be found. And she doesn't answer her phone. She is not going to get away with this. The judge agreed to send a deputy sheriff to serve her a warrant immediately." Randy paced. "Damn her!" He slammed his file down on the plaintiff's table as he barreled out of the courtroom. Gerard called an hour recess.

Anne decided to wait until Bryan could confirm his information before saying anything to Randy. She used the time to catch up on transcription. She couldn't imagine why Stephanie would risk incurring the Court's wrath by not showing up. Maybe she had flown to the Caymans without Sherman. Maybe, while Sherman sweated it out in court, she was emptying his offshore account. Maybe she would pick up a lifeguard and live on love and margaritas for the rest of her life. *Tim deserved it.* Anne jumped when the phone rang, knocking it to the floor. Visions of sand and surf vanished.

"Hey, doll, the Judge wants everyone back in court," Gerard said.

"Did Stephanie show up?"

"Not exactly. You better get here."

Way to go, Stephanie! Anne felt certain that Stephanie was lying hip to hip with her lover *du jour* on a sun-drenched beach. *What are secret offshore accounts for, if not to share?*

In the courtroom, she made eye contact with Randy. Distress etched his face. With Stephanie

AWOL, Randy lacked the evidence he needed. He would lose the case. Anne glanced at Sherman's attorneys. They were fumbling with their files and avoiding eye contact. Judge Johnston, already on the bench, motioned for Anne to begin. The scene had a feeling of unreality. The judge cleared his throat.

"At the request of Mrs. Sherman's attorneys, and with the agreement of Mr. Sherman's attorneys, the trial will be continued for one week." A buzz filled the courtroom. "That should give Mr. Sherman heartburn," Anne thought.

The judge continued. "I am sorry to have to announce that Stephanie Burke, a material witness in this case, has been murdered." Anne's fingers froze. Her heart lodged in her throat. Breathing became difficult. *Murdered! Oh my God!* Anne tried to digest it. Her mind raced. *How could this happen?* Anne glanced at Randy. His face was ghostly. He shook his head and lowered his eyes. *The plan was for Stephanie to spill the beans. The plan did not include murder.* Anne tried to move but could not.

"Ms. Marshall? Ms. Marshall? Are you all right?"

Anne strained to hear the judge and process his words.

Anne willed herself to nod.

"Yes, your Honor. I'm fine," she whispered. She glanced around the courtroom. Everyone was staring at her. "Yes, yes, I'm all right," she repeated a bit louder. "I'm sorry, could you repeat the last sentence?" He did, then called a recess. Anne sat dazed as the courtroom emptied. She looked across the room where Gerard gathered his papers. He looked up at Anne and shook his head. She turned toward Randy.

"Let's go to the Jury Room and get some coffee," he said. Anne nodded.

They walked in silence. Randy guided Anne past the bar to a booth.

"Ohmygod, Randy! What happened?"

"Here's what I know." He was deliberate with his words as if he did not want Anne, or anyone else, jumping to conclusions.

"As you know, when Stephanie didn't show up for court this morning, I requested that a Deputy be sent to bring her in."

"Oh for God's sake," Anne snapped, "I know that. Get to the point."

Randy flashed her a cautionary look. "Cool your jets. I'm trying to tell you what happened."

"Okay, okay." She picked at a hangnail then searched her purse for a pencil to gnaw on.

"When the Deputy got to Stephanie's he didn't get a response. He went around to the front window for a better look."

"And?" Anne interrupted. She couldn't stand the way he dragged things out.

"And," Randy continued more slowly, "the Deputy noticed that the living room had been ransacked–sufficiently to justify entering the house. He tried the back door. It was unlocked. As soon as he went in, he saw Stephanie on the kitchen floor lying in a pool of blood, no doubt her own. Her head had been bashed in. The Deputy determined she was dead and called it in."

Anne sat back in the booth. "It must have been—"

Randy cut her off. "We must be very careful and not jump to conclusions we can't support."

"You know what I am thinking, don't you?"

"If you think Sherman did this to keep her quiet, then, yes that's what I'm thinking."

"If Sherman did it, how do we prove it?" Before Randy could answer, Anne hit the table with a clenched fist. "That bastard's not going to get away with this."

"I agree, Anne, but we have to play by the rules. Let's wait for the coroner's report. We have to know the time of death to be able to track Sherman's movements."

Anne nodded. "You're right. Any idea when that will be?"

"Sheriff Collins said maybe tomorrow. He asked Doc Claremont to make it a priority."

"Did the Sheriff say anything else?"

"From what I was told, it is being treated as a homicide. At this point they're guessing the motive was robbery since several items were missing–a DVR, television, jewelry, and other personal possessions. The back door was busted. All consistent with a robbery."

Anne listened carefully. "Sherman would want it to look like a robbery, wouldn't he?"

"He would. Let's make sure there's proof before we go off." They sat there conjecturing and didn't notice Jason until he slid into the booth next to Anne. She jumped.

"Not the kind of response a guy wants from his girl," he teased.

"You startled me."

"If I were the jealous type, I'd wonder what you two were up to." Anne started to protest. She was not in the mood for humor, even Jason's. "I heard about your key witness. Knowing Anne's fertile imagination, I figured you two were solving the crime." He turned to Randy. "Bad luck about your case."

Randy shook his head, "Worse than you know." Randy filled him in and Anne editorialized. "We both think Tim Sherman did it," Anne said. Randy nodded affirmatively.

"Not you too, Randy," Jason said in disbelief. "Has Anne convinced you of this offshore account nonsense?"

"I agree with Anne. All reason points to it, but we can't prove it."

"That reminds me," Anne broke in, "My friend Bryan thinks he knows something. He's just waiting to confirm it."

Jason looked incredulous. "Anne, you're already conspiring with Randy. That's shaky enough. Now you've involved Bryan?"

Anne quickly defended herself. "I didn't involve Bryan. He read about it in the newspaper and knew I was the reporter on the case."

Jason gave a sigh. "The two of you may be right about this offshore thing. You're more involved in this case than I am. But now we have a murder. Don't jump to conclusions. Be careful. You are on very dangerous ground, my friends."

"You are so right," Randy said. "Though it's hard not to."

"Anne," Jason cautioned, "remember, you are an officer of the court. That may give you access unavailable to others, but–and this is a big but–you also have a greater responsibility as well."

Anne knew he was right. But her gut told her to utilize all privileges her job afforded her.

Randy excused himself. "I have to go. Call you if I hear anything more."

Jason turned to Anne. "Since you don't have class tonight, I thought we could do something."

"Why, Mr. Perry, are you suggesting what I think you are?" Anne asked with a coy smile, tossing her hair. "If that's what you're suggesting, I'm looking forward to it."

"You always could read me."

"I'm meeting my study group at five, but I'll be home by nine. Do you think you'll be up to it?" She teased.

"Always up for a challenge," he grinned.

She paused for a minute. What if her dad was there? They certainly had a lot to talk about. She backtracked. "Why don't we say ten o'clock?"

"It's never too late for you." He gave her a quick kiss on the cheek. They got up and walked together to the courthouse.

In the lobby, Jason turned left for the elevators to criminal court. "I'll see you tonight, and be careful," he called as the doors closed. As soon as he was out of view, Anne tore down the steps to the county morgue. The smells of formaldehyde and other unpleasant bodily fluids assaulted her. The stench became stronger the closer she came to her destination. She wondered why a doctor would choose this as a profession. Dr. Claremont, the Coroner, had told her that being a forensic pathologist was like writing a novel. Each body told its own story; unraveling that story was his masterpiece. *To each his own.*

Anne entered and spotted Dr. Claremont standing beside a cadaver laid out on the table. She had known Dr. Claremont most of her life. He had been a close friend of her father's and had a soft spot where Anne was concerned. At one time Anne had considered medical school and Dr. Claremont had been thrilled. Yet he understood when she decided on the law.

Anne looked around. Business was booming. She counted three bodies awaiting autopsies. Terry, one of Dr. Claremont's assistants, waved her over.

A second later he pulled the sheet off a white male in his early fifties. He reached down and pulled his cart full of instruments closer to the corpse.

"What brings you down our way?"

"I'm interested in the Stephanie Burke case."

"Over here," Dr. Claremont signaled as he turned to greet Anne. Blood covered his gown. Small patches of white showed through.

"Perfect timing, Anne. I'm working on her now. What's your interest?"

Anne walked over to the table and tried not to look directly at the corpse. No matter how many times she had been down here, she never got used to autopsies. She fixed her gaze at Dr. Claremont's nose.

"I'm the court reporter on this case. I am really interested in what happened."

"Anything in particular?" He peered over the top of his glasses at her.

"Not sure. What about the time of death? Have you determined that?"

The doctor hesitated. Anne could see he was considering how to answer.

"Well, best I can determine, it was somewhere

between midnight and three in the morning. That help you at all?”

“That certainly narrows it down.” *Where was Sherman between midnight and 3:00 a.m.?*

“Looks pretty straightforward. Blow to the head. Enough to kill her on impact. Probably a man.”

Aha. Now we are getting someplace.

“Someone broke open the back door. Maybe she knew him, maybe not. It’s clear there was a struggle because there was bruising on her wrist and arms.” Dr. Claremont added.

“Was she hit from the front or from behind?” Anne asked.

“From behind. It looks like she had broken free and turned, maybe to run, but we will never know. It appears she was hit with a mallet, the kind you use to tenderize meat. The crosshatch marks on the skull are very distinctive. When they searched, the police didn’t find it in her kitchen, so the killer may have taken it with him. Anything else?” He turned back to the body. She watched as he lifted out the liver and placed it on the scale.

Bile rose in Anne’s throat. She feared gagging– or worse. *I really need to go.* “No, thanks. Don’t need anything else.” On her way out she called over her shoulder, "You have been very helpful, Doc. As usual, I owe you one."

"I intend to collect, preferably in the form of cookies." She took the steps two at a time. She knew it would take her all night to get rid of the morgue smell. The memory of Stephanie Burke's liver being lifted onto a scale would take longer. She wasted no time getting on an elevator to the third floor. Soon as she stepped out, Shirley confronted her–as if she'd been waiting all day.

"Anne, I'm glad I've found you. Would you be a dear and fill in for Courtroom C? I don't know how we are going to cope with this flu going around." Anne guessed that it was more a plea then a question.

"Of course, Shirley, glad to."

Shirley gave a sigh of relief then darted off after another court reporter. Anne felt grateful that her job was less complicated than Shirley's. Anne was assigned to only one courtroom at a time while Shirley had the entire courthouse to administer. *What a nightmare!*

In Courtroom C, a minor dispute was settled during a break. Anne finished her work and left to rendezvous with her law school study group.

Anne couldn't wait to share the news with Maria. A crackerjack homicide detective would tell her in which direction to head. The evidence was clear. The perp had been a man. He killed her. Sherman probably confronted Stephanie about her impending testimony. She had been furious about his betrayal. She threatened to tell the court about his offshore account. They struggled. He grabbed the meat tenderizer and crushed her skull. He messed up the house to make it look like a break-in. Case closed. What might Anne do to get the police to arrest Sherman? If anyone had the answers, Maria would.

Anne headed for the lunchroom, the first to arrive. Bryan came in soon after. Before he'd taken off his coat, he began yammering.

"I hear your key witness was murdered last night. That was your case, wasn't it? Stephanie Burke?" Anne opened her mouth to respond but he plowed on. "Don't you think it's a little coincidental that she was murdered before she could turn on him?"

Anne had heard enough and jumped in. "I think it's too much of a coincidence. I think Tim Sherman is guilty as hell. Now, how to prove it. I hope Maria can help with that."

As if on cue, Maria walked in. Anne and Bryan started babbling at the same time.

"Put a lid on it. I know what this is about. We need to take this one at a time—starting with me." Anne did her best to interrupt. Maria held up her hand. "Let's be methodical. Let's not jump to conclusions." Maria fixed Anne in her crosshairs.

"First," Maria continued. "I assume the murder victim, Stephanie Burke, is the same Stephanie Burke that we were discussing yesterday." Anne started to speak. Maria held up her STOP sign again. "A yes or no nod is all that is required right now." Anne nodded. Anne looked to Bryan who nodded affirmatively.

"This is not my case. Shane is handling this one," Maria continued. "So I have the same information you can read in the newspaper. I do know the Coroner feels it was a man, which might be Tim Sherman, right?" Bryan and Anne nodded.

"Tim Sherman has motive because of the scene in the courtroom and the fact that Ms. Burke may have information he did not want revealed. Right?" Bryan and Anne agreed. "And finally, he had opportunity. So, he may be the prime suspect–motive, opportunity and means."

Anne could not contain herself. "That's what I think! So when are they going to arrest him?"

"They aren't."

"What?" Anne's mouth gaped. "What do you mean they're not arresting him?"

"Anne, jumping to conclusions without the hard evidence to back it up could blow the entire case. However, I can tell you that Sherman is the prime suspect. He is being brought in for questioning. In the meantime, they're following up *all* leads."

Anne threw up her hands in exasperation. "Okay, I give. I'll let you do your job. But believe me, he's guilty as hell."

"Why is everyone so intense?" Clark asked. He and John approached with a pizza, steam rising from the box. That broke the tension as they clamored for slices. Maria and Anne brought the newcomers up to speed. The group broke about eight thirty. Anne looked at her watch and called Jason. He answered on the second ring.

"Hi, sweetie," he said, "all finished?"

"Sure am. Slight change of plans. I'm heading home for some clothes then I'll come over there. Crack open a bottle of wine. I should be there in an hour." She wanted ample time to talk to her father.

When she entered her apartment she didn't see her father and she didn't smell pipe tobacco. "Oh great," she thought. "Just when I needed to talk to him."

His voice from the kitchen startled her and she jumped.

"I'm here, Angel. This is a nasty situation. I never expected Tim to react so violently." Anne watched his silhouette pacing between the sink and refrigerator.

"Please stop pacing and talk to me." He sat down at the table. "You know about Stephanie's murder?"

"Of course. I was at the courthouse and heard the news. I was in absolute shock." It had never occurred to Anne that her father was out and about during the day. Then she reminded herself that he could not have messed up her transcript and known about courthouse goings on unless he was out and about. She wondered what ghosts did all day. One thing was certain, they had plenty of time in which to do it.

"What I can't understand is why he would murder her. He's smart enough to know that he'd be the first person they'd suspect."

"I don't think he considered that," Anne jumped in. "I think his desire to keep her quiet overtook him. I'm sure he's guilty and I'm going to make sure he gets what's coming to him." Anne grabbed a bottle of water out of the refrigerator. She offered it to her dad, then realized the absurdity of it and kept it for herself.

"I agree with you, Angel. If he did this, we need to make sure he is held responsible. But how?"

"Exactly." Anne filled him in on what she had learned from the Coroner and how Maria said Sherman was being brought in for questioning. As they rehashed, a strange feeling came over her that something didn't add up. They needed more proof. Anne glanced at the clock. It was ten.

"Sorry, dad. Jason is expecting me. I have to go. I will visit Stephanie's neighborhood tomorrow and see if I can discover anything."

"Good idea. And, by the way, when are you two getting married?"

"Gotta run!" she called over her shoulder and dashed out the door. *Close call.*

Jason met her at his front door and kissed her. "I was getting worried."

"Sorry, time got away from me." She went to the kitchen and poured them wine. He followed her in and wrapped his arms around her waist. Then he buried his face in her hair.

"Um, that feels so good." She turned and threw her arms around his neck. "Really good," she whispered, and pressed her lips against his wonderful mouth. They never drank the wine.

•••••••

Celia accosted Bryan as soon as he walked in. "Were you able to find anything useful in the documents Alice gave you?"

"I think I may have. When I was looking at his revenue and his client list, I noticed a large chunk of revenue missing, specifically Statton Industries. My old accounting firm lost them to none other than Tim Sherman about two years ago. I remember because it was a large account. The annual fees were over six figures. Sherman's records indicated Mr. Statton paid less than $10,000. I called Roger, and he confirmed the fees and that Statton was still with Sherman. Roger had tried to woo Statton back, but he said he was happy and wasn't leaving Sherman. I don't think anyone else would have picked up on that."

"Is that enough to prove Sherman has an offshore account?"

"That doesn't prove he has an offshore account. If they subpoena Mr. Statton it will help prove Tim is lying about his revenue. That may be enough. I'll share this with Anne tomorrow."

"Good work, eagle-eye." She teased. "That deserves some of my homemade apple pie."

"Is that all?" he asked as he reached for her hand.

•••••••

Tim Sherman sat in his office, his hands twitching. His mouth was dry as cotton. He poured himself a scotch. He was smart enough to know that the cops would suspect him. *How could such a perfect plan implode so quickly?* He thought about the last few nights. Stephanie was key to finalizing his divorce settlement. Why did he call Gloria? How dumb was that? He never suspected his wife was having him followed. He thought they were way past that. This mess was not his fault. He had been under a lot of stress. He needed the diversion of a hot woman like Gloria. How could he have anticipated Stephanie's reaction? She always was a little deranged. No, this was not his fault. Now the cops would be dragging him in for questioning. He knew it. He had to stay calm. Think. The best defense is a good offense. He picked up the telephone and dialed his attorney. They needed to head this off now. Keep him out of the heat and get the divorce over. They are getting paid enough. It's their job to clean up this mess! He'd be fine. It'll work out.

Then he heard the knock on the door. He dropped his scotch.

9

Sherman was sitting in the police interrogation room waiting for his attorney. *Where the hell is that high paid sonofabitch?*

Detectives Shane O'Malley and Rick Bridges sat across from him. O'Malley tapped his empty coffee cup with his pen. Tap. Tap. Tap.

"I'm not saying a word until my attorney gets here."

"We've got all night," O'Malley affirmed. "How about some coffee?"

"You think I'm crazy? You fill me full of coffee and keep me from the bathroom. I watch TV. I know your tricks."

"You're really on to us," Det. Bridges said with a smirk. *Who does this guy think he is?*

"Just tell us where you were the night of Stephanie Burke's murder, between the hours of

11:00 p.m. and three in the morning, and this whole thing can be cleared up." O'Malley goaded.

"You got something in your ears? I told you, I'm not talking."

"Fine with us," Bridges said. Tap. Tap. Tap.

The door flew open and Attorney Norm Reece stomped in. "My client has nothing to say." He grabbed Sherman by the arm. "Come on. We're out of here."

Sherman got up.

"Hold on. We aren't finished with Mr. Sherman." Det. O'Malley threatened.

"Oh, but you are." Sherman took a step toward the door.

"It looks to me like Mr. Sherman is afraid to tell us where he was the night of Stephanie Burke's murder. Sounds like a guilty man. What do you think, Det. Bridges?"

"That's what it looks like to me too. Only a guilty man wouldn't answer the question. I think we need to investigate further. And tell your client not to leave town until this investigation is over."

Sherman panicked. He felt beads of sweat building on his forehead. "Wait a minute. If I tell you where I was last night, can I go?"

"Absolutely," O'Malley assured him.

"I have to caution you, Mr. Sherman. Don't tell them anything," his attorney warned.

"I have nothing to hide. Sure, I was with Stephanie. We had dinner at La Petite Fleur. That's her favorite restaurant. She was a little upset with me."

"We hear she was furious with you and attacked you in open court." O'Malley said.

"That was a misunderstanding. She agreed to meet me for dinner so we could patch things up. Stephanie is . . . was a little high strung. That was all. We left the restaurant a little after 11:00 p.m. She went her way and I went mine. I was home and in bed by eleven thirty. You can check it out."

"Oh, we intend to." Bridges promised.

"You got my client's alibi. We're leaving." Mr. Reece grabbed Sherman's shoulder and the two started for the door.

"Don't leave town," O'Malley cautioned.

Sherman could feel the veins puffing up in his neck. He shouted, "What the hell?"

Reece grabbed Sherman's arm and pushed him out the door. "We're done."

Det. O'Malley looked at Det. Bridges. "Well— that went well."

Bridges laughed. "Funny, I never pictured him

a pipe smoker."

"You picked up on the pipe tobacco smell too?"

Bridges shook his head. "Let's check out his alibi. In the mood for French food?"

"Oui, oui." O'Malley grabbed his notepad and followed Bridges.

•••••••

Jim Marshall watched the interrogation with interest. Sherman was clearly shaken, yet he seemed confident about his alibi. That would be easy enough for Det. O'Malley to check out. The two detectives were heading to the restaurant now. Marshall had to find out if Sherman murdered Stephanie Burke. When he started this, Marshall never imagined it would go so far. *What have I started? What have I gotten Anne into?*

•••••••

Anne awoke to the aroma of coffee. She liked having someone to make her morning coffee. Living alone, it was one of the things she missed. She rolled over and stretched. The sun streamed in, creating stripes on the wall. She sniffed the pillow and thought about how lucky she was. Jason came in bearing two mugs.

"Oh, is Sleeping Beauty awake?"

"Awake and deliriously happy," she replied before taking a sip.

"Well, I'm here to please." He winked, kissed her forehead and disappeared into the bathroom. Anne could hear the shower running as she slipped out of bed and into the shower with Jason.

"Well, hello there." He grinned and pulled her closer, kissing her neck.

It had been their first weekend in ages. Anne savored it. Saturday night they ordered pizza and rented a movie. Sunday morning Anne went to her apartment for fresh clothes. No sign of her father–which was okay with her. She needed to step back and take a breath. *This can all wait until Monday.*

Monday morning came too soon, ending their tranquil time together. Anne left before Jason and drove to the courthouse garage. She found a spot and walked to her office where she scanned the day's schedule. Shirley Williams' efficiency had triumphed again.

Anne spent the morning in Courtroom B on a

domestic case. Over lunch, Gerard told her there was nothing new on the Sherman case. Sherman had been brought in for questioning Friday night, but as far as Gerard knew, he was not being held.

"Well, that's some progress," she said.

With a couple of hours before her six o'clock class, Anne drove the ten minutes to Stephanie's neighborhood. The houses were moderately expensive and well kept. She checked the address she had pulled from the court records: 517 Cherry Court. She read the numbers neatly stenciled on the curb as she drove by at a crawl. Half way down the block she found Stephanie's house–a pretty little Cape Cod with immaculate landscaping. It wasn't what she had expected. Sherman must have covered the expenses. She parked across the street and surveyed the neighborhood. *Where to start?* She'd have to rely on what she saw on *Law & Order* or *CSI* where there was always someone walking a dog. And the requisite nosy neighbor.

A woman in her late fifties was on her hands and knees weeding a flowerbed. *Perfect.* Anne walked toward the woman and pulled out her court ID badge. The woman got up. She eyed Anne suspiciously. "Show time," Anne thought.

She smiled and flashed her ID.

"Good morning. I'm with the prosecutor's office. I'm investigating the Stephanie Burke murder and wondered if I could have a moment with you?" Anne couldn't believe her own ears. Well, it was half-true. She wasn't with the Prosecutor's office, but she had been with a Prosecutor last night. *Close enough.* The woman relaxed.

"I guess I have a minute."

"Can we begin with your name?" Anne took out a small notebook. *Very professional.*

"Of course, dear." The woman smiled. "My name is Clara Richman, and I've lived here for almost fifteen years." She hesitated. "No, I didn't see anything the night poor Stephanie was murdered. I go to bed early, watch the news and Jay Leno in my bedroom. Poor dear. Stephanie, not Jay Leno." Anne smiled to put the woman at ease.

"I guess you've had a lot of questions within the last several days. Bear with me a few minutes longer. We appreciate your help."

Anne got the feeling that Mrs. Richman enjoyed the attention and the excitement. Anne continued. "I am interested in Ms. Burke's friends. Did she have many visitors, any family?"

Mrs. Richman finger-tapped her lip. "Not a lot of visitors. Just her boss, Mr. Sherman. He seemed like such a nice man." Anne let this pass. "I think she had a sister who lived down south, Alabama or Mississippi. She did have a nephew, her sister's boy. I didn't see either of them around here much. Stephanie would go there for holidays. She was real close to them. Talked about them all the time and always showed me pictures. She sent them money, you know."

"Was Mr. Sherman here often? Do you recall if he was here the night she was murdered?"

Mrs. Richman took her time before answering. "He was here often enough, if you know what I mean." She winked and nudged Anne with her elbow. "But I didn't see him here that night. In fact she was out. She hadn't come home when I went to bed at eleven. I always look out my window to check the street before I turn in. There were no lights on at her house." Anne thanked the woman and returned to her car.

If Stephanie was out that night, where had she been–and with whom? A quick glance up and down the street told her no one else was around. She pulled out and headed for class.

Anne hoped to corral Maria to see if the police had made any progress. Anne was the last of the study group to arrive. The others had taken on the Stephanie Burke murder case as a team project and were eager for new information. Maria exercised control over the wannabe detectives by not compromising the case. She volunteered only general information.

John greeted Anne, "Welcome to our sleuth group." Anne pulled up a chair and dropped her books on the table.

"Maria, any progress?"

"They brought Tim Sherman in for questioning. He admitted they were having an affair and that he was with Ms. Burke the night she was murdered. They met for dinner. There were plenty of witnesses to verify they went their separate ways around eleven thirty that night. Sherman said he assumed she was going home."

Okay, that jives with the neighbor's take. Stephanie was not home by eleven. Sherman could have followed her home. Anne hesitated to share what she had learned.

"Maria," Anne said cautiously. "I ran into one of Stephanie's neighbors."

"Ran into?" Maria's dark eyes flashed.

"Yes, I ran into Clara Richman." Anne looked away. "I believe she lives across the street from Stephanie." Anne expected flames to shoot from Maria's mouth. "She said that Stephanie didn't have many visitors, just Tim Sherman. She also said Stephanie had a sister and a nephew down south, family she was really close to. And she sent them money." Anne paused and waited for Maria's wrath.

"Let's go over the part about you running into Stephanie's neighbor," Maria said through clenched teeth. Bryan, John, and Clark pushed away from the table. They appeared eager to escape any fallout.

"I drove by. Just curious—" Anne's voice trailed off. "She happened to be in her front yard. Planting flowers."

Maria shook her head.

"Will you let us do our jobs? Do not mess up this case or we'll both be very unhappy. We already know about the sister and the nephew. They seem to be Stephanie's only next of kin. We are checking them out and I will keep you posted. Now, can we move on?"

Anne took a deep breath.

Outside the classroom, Bryan pulled Anne

aside. "I think I may have the missing link."

Anne ushered Bryan into a corner. "What did you find?" Her heart raced.

"I noticed that Sherman grossly understated revenue from Statton Industries. That account is worth over six figures and he booked it at $10,000. Mr. Statton will have to testify as to his real fees if subpoenaed."

"That just proves Sherman is lying about his revenue."

"But the question then becomes, where is the money?"

Anne considered this. "Bryan, I think you are right. Can you get me a copy so I can get it to Randy Vers?"

"I have it right here." He handed Anne a file.

"This may prove he hid money, but what about poor Stephanie? He murdered her and I have to prove it."

"This may prove motive. If Stephanie knew and threatened to expose him, he would have reason to kill her." Bryan offered.

"Thanks, Bryan." Anne slipped the file into her notebook.

•••••••

Tension filled the air. Professor Craft preyed on victim after victim. Tonight, it was worse. With her thoughts on Sherman, Anne could barely pay attention. She opened a package of peanut butter crackers to munch on–an effort to avoid wood-chomping. Although Homicide was handling the case, it wasn't good enough for Anne. In some convoluted way, she felt responsible for Stephanie's death. She was the one who had set the events in motion. It was her actions that had led to Stephanie's brutal murder. In her mind, she was the one who had to do something. But what? The information she had gathered from the neighbor was useful, but Homicide already had it. Maybe there was something in Stephanie's house or on her computer that the police had missed. Info about the offshore account. Maybe Sherman dropped a cufflink. Her gut told her there must be something the police overlooked. She wouldn't rest until she investigated further.

After class, Anne grabbed John. With him came his Siamese twin, Clark. Then Bryan walked by and wanted in. Anne motioned them into a corner. She had seen Maria rush from the building and get into her car. "Thank God," she thought. What she wanted John to do was better discussed away from Maria.

"John, I have an idea and I need your help," Anne started.

"Anything, what is it?"

"I was thinking. If we can find some evidence against Tim Sherman, we can nail him." She waited for John's reaction.

"What kind of information? And why do you need me?" John asked.

"If we can get into Stephanie's computer, we may find something. I don't have a clue how to break into a computer. That's where you come in."

"Sure, I can do that. Where is it?"

"That's the problem."

"What problem?"

"It's still at her house." There, she had said it. She felt relieved.

"Still at her house?"

"We'll have to break into her computer."

"And how would we do that? Are you saying we have to break into her house?" John backed away. Clark and Bryan jumped. "Anne, are you nuts?"

"Guys, I feel responsible for this poor woman's death. I can't let it rest. Please help me." she pleaded.

John spoke first. "I'm up for a little excitement. When do we go?"

"No time like the present," Anne replied.

John turned to Clark. "I don't want you involved. This could be dangerous."

"No way I'm letting you have all the fun. This reminds me of college when we broke into the Dean's office and hot glued his stapler and phone to his desk. I'm in. Besides you need a lookout."

"Are you sure?" Anne and John asked. Clark nodded.

"What about me?" Bryan asked. "Do you know anything about offshore accounts?" He looked at their blank faces. "I didn't think so, so I'm in too." He gave Anne a knowing look. "I'm already more involved than I should be. No reason to pull out now."

John and Clark glanced at each other, then to Anne and Bryan. "What does he mean by that?"

"It's not important. Are you in or not?" Bryan asked.

John made it official. "We're in. I guess the sleuth group is on the case." They high-fived each other and swore secrecy.

"Let's go in my car," Anne offered. "One car won't draw as much attention." They piled into Anne's coupe and took off.

She turned onto Cherry Court. They looked for any suspicious characters–or the police who might find the merry band of would-be detectives suspicious. Anne pulled behind Stephanie's house and withdrew a flashlight from the glove compartment. They crept silently to the back of the house. Police tape stretched across the door.

"Is this going to be a problem?" John asked.

"I don't think so," Anne replied with more confidence than she felt. She tried the doorknob. Locked. Clark stepped forward.

"I have always wanted to try this." He pulled a credit card from his wallet and slid it between the door and the lock. The lock clicked. The door opened with ease. Before going in they did a quick sweep to be sure they hadn't been spotted. A street lamp provided dim illumination inside. Anne took the flashlight from her pocket.

"Sheeesh!" screeched Clark.

"You just screamed like a girl." John chided.

"There is something slimy on the floor."

Anne clicked on the flashlight.

"Ohmygod!" John gasped. "It's blood!

"No one panic!" Anne whispered in a shaky voice. "They haven't cleaned up the crime scene yet. Just ignore it. They tell me you get used to it."

"I doubt that," Clark mumbled.

Anne looked around and grabbed a roll of paper towels from the counter and handed it to Clark. "Wipe your shoes off. We don't want you to leave bloody footprints. Everyone else be careful. Let's see if we can find her computer and get out of here."

In the living room's eerie glow, Anne, Bryan, and John combed every inch. Anne felt like an intruder. She knew deep down she shouldn't be there. But nothing would stand in her way. She must find something that would nail Sherman.

"Anne, give me the flashlight," John said. "There's a hallway off the living room. Her computer may be in one of the bedrooms." He motioned for them to follow to a bedroom that had been converted into an office.

"Voila!" John flashed the light on the computer. Anne, Clark, and Bryan followed on John's heels. Anne drew the shades on the lone window and shut the door halfway. John turned on the desk lamp and sat down.

"Do your magic, John," Anne coached. With a grin, he held up his hands and wiggled his fingers –a magician poised to pull a rabbit out of a hat.

Anne smacked him on the back of his head.

"All right. All right. Can't a guy warm up first?" John laughed. He turned the computer on and watched the programs load. Anne looked around the room. The office was very tidy. The desk was facing the window. Bookcases lined one wall. Photographs filled the shelves. In one, Stephanie and Sherman were arm in arm on a beach. They looked blissful. Maybe he really did love her. It was apparent from the way she looked at him that she really loved him. Reality intruded, squelching Anne's pleasant thoughts about Sherman. *The bastard.*

"Okay, it's booted up." John announced. "Now, any clue what her password might be?"

They all looked at each other. "Isn't that what you're here for?" Bryan asked.

"If we had all night, I could eventually get in, but we don't. I could use your input."

Anne walked over to John. "I don't have a clue."

"Passwords are usually familiar names or dates," John offered. "Like the name of a pet or relative or birth date. Something easy to remember."

Anne thought for a minute. She wished she had looked at the case file for Stephanie's birth date.

"Try her name. Try Tim's name." Anne offered. John tried some of the common words, then some tricks only computer geeks know. Anne resumed looking at the pictures.

"Most of the pictures were taken in the Islands. Maybe her password is related."

"I'm trying," John said. "So far, no luck."

Clark picked up a photo of a cat. "What's this?" Hmm. *Fluffycat* is engraved in the frame. Try that."

"Good idea." John tapped the keyboard. "Bingo. I'm in. Way to go, Clark."

"I knew I was good for something."

"Hey, I thought you were going to be our lookout," Bryan chided.

"Oops, forgot." Clark opened the door a tad and slipped into the hall.

"Now that you are in, let me take a look," Bryan said. He and John traded places. To Anne, it seemed like forever as Bryan scanned hundreds of Stephanie's files. "I see lots of personal stuff but no account information or corporate names."

"Try her e-mails," Anne suggested. John took the helm from Bryan. A minute later they were scanning Stephanie's e-mails.

"It looks like Sherman e-mailed her the day

of her outburst in court," John said. Anne looked over John's shoulder.

"Boy was he scrambling to get back in her good graces," Anne said. "This one pleads with her to meet him for dinner–so he can explain." Anne hit the desk with her fist. "Damn that jerk! Look at this garbage. He says he loves her. He says he was set up by Isabelle. Gimme a break. Isabelle had nothing to do with his womanizing!"

"Anne, calm down." John took her hand. "We are here to find something to nail this guy. We can't get emotional or we may miss something."

"You're right." Anne pulled her hand away.

"According to Maria, Stephanie did meet him, so that makes sense. Are there any other e-mails?" Anne asked.

"Nothing of importance," John said.

The three of them stood there saying nothing.

"What shall we do next? I'm at a loss," Anne said.

Clark opened the door enough to whisper that a cruiser was passing the house–very slowly. John turned off the lamp. Anne hoped that since the office was in the back of the house, the police wouldn't notice the light. They froze. Anne could feel her heart pounding in her chest. Her palms started to sweat. *What had she done? And why had she dragged her friends into this?* She put her index finger to her lips to silence everyone. She squeezed through the office door, dropping to a crouch in the hallway. She could see through the living room window and watched the cruiser slow to a near stop. The officer shined his flashlight across the front of the house. No one moved. The officer turned off his flashlight and continued down the street. When the cruiser had turned the corner, Anne issued an "all clear."

"Phew. That was close," John said. "I'm having trouble breathing."

"My feelings exactly," Bryan echoed.

"I don't think I would look good in an orange jumpsuit," Clark added. "Not my color."

John jumped in. "I don't think there's anything here on this computer to help you. If there is, I can't find it–and I'm pretty good."

"You're probably right. It was worth a shot," Anne said. "I've put all of you to a lot of trouble. Let's call it a night."

Anne led the way back through the living room. "Careful in the kitchen," she cautioned. Nobody asked what she meant. They slipped out the back door, across the lawn, and into Anne's car. Anne had the distinct feeling that someone was watching them. A few minutes later she pulled into the law school parking lot, dropped off her friends, and drove off.

"I recognize that beach," Anne's father said from the passenger seat. Anne slammed on the brakes and hit her shoulder on the door.

"Stop scaring me! Is there some way you can announce your presence before you speak?"

"Sorry, Angel. This is new to me as well."

"I'm a little jumpy. Sorry I snapped. Breaking and entering is hardly old hat to me."

"It's okay, Anne."

"What do you mean you recognize that beach?"

"There was a hotel in the background. Your mother and I spent a vacation there years ago. I recognize the beach and the hotel."

"Do you think that's where the offshore account is?"

"Very possibly. I think you need to pass the information on to Randy. Maybe he can check it out."

"At least it's something to go on. It may give the authorities reason to go light on me when I'm arrested for compromising a crime scene."

•••••••

Maria slammed the front door behind her. She threw her books on the table. Half of them slid onto the floor. "Dammit." She stooped to pick them up. "You are not going to believe what Anne has done now." She didn't wait for her husband to answer. "She went to Stephanie Burke's neighborhood and started questioning the neighbors."

"What?" Shane jumped off the couch. "Is she insane?"

"She's obsessed. She could jeopardize this entire investigation." Maria was pacing. "This is your case. What are you going to do?"

"I have to warn her off. This is a murder case. She is interfering with a police investigation. I could have her arrested."

"It might serve her right." Maria dropped into her chair. "I don't know what to do with her. Anne and Jason are two of our best friends. You can't arrest her."

"You know I won't, but she can't continue to interfere. I'll talk to her. It's better coming from me than from you."

Maria agreed. She lifted her feet onto the hassock and gave a big sigh. *Anne what are you doing?*

• • • • • • •

Tim Sherman sat in his living room sipping his fifth scotch. *That bitch Stephanie has messed up everything.* The police had held him for over two hours. But he had his alibi. Nosiree, they weren't going to nail him on this one. At least with Stephanie out of the way he would be free to wrap up the divorce and leave this god-forsaken place. But they said he couldn't leave town. *Damn that woman! Damn, damn, damn!* He got up and poured another scotch.

10

Exhausted and fearful, Anne unlocked her door with a trembling hand. Once inside, she locked the door, then checked it again. She pushed the flashing button on her phone and heard her mother's soothing voice. Ah, an invitation for Jason and her to a cookout on Saturday. Randy and Ilene Vers would be there too. Anne smiled. The timing for a pleasant diversion couldn't be better. And it would give her an opportunity to compare notes with Randy.

She looked around for her father, wishing she had the power to summon him. He had disappeared before she could tell him what she had learned that day. She called Jason to invite him to the cookout. When she mentioned that Randy would be there, Anne heard his voice perk up. Clearly he took a bigger interest in the Sherman case than he let on. She hung up and flopped on the couch, turned on the TV, and promptly fell asleep.

"Anne, Angel, wake up. We have to talk."

Her head jerked at hearing her father's voice. "You bet we have to talk. What happened to you? I wanted to tell you what I found out today."

"You go first," he said and took his usual seat in the high-backed chair. Anne shared the news about the revenue from Statton Industries and that Tim Sherman had been brought in for questioning.

"I have information too. I was at the police station while they were interrogating Tim. The night Stephanie was murdered, she met him at that fancy French restaurant downtown."

"Le Petite Fleur?"

"That's the one."

"Go on, I want every juicy detail."

"After questioning Sherman, Shane and Det. Rick Bridges talked to the waitstaff at the restaurant. One of the waitresses remembered Sherman and Burke and said they had quite a row. They left the restaurant around eleven thirty, still fighting. The parking valet said Stephanie Burke was screaming and very agitated. Tim and Stephanie got in their cars and drove off in opposite directions."

"Then he might have followed her home," Anne said. "I bet he did."

Her father nodded. "That's what I thought. However, the police verified with Tim's neighbors that he pulled into his garage around 11:30. They saw the lights go out and nothing more after that."

"Damn. His alibi is getting tighter." Anne drummed her fingers on the coffee table. "Stephanie was murdered between midnight and 3:00 a.m. Sherman could have slipped out unseen after midnight. We have to prove that he went out later."

"Exactly." Her father rose and started to pace, tapping his pipe on his chin.

"Any ideas?" Anne asked.

He shook his head. "None at all."

Anne got up with a start. "This isn't getting us anywhere. It's been a long day and I'm whipped. Let's sleep on it. Maybe we'll have an idea in the morning." With that she grabbed her bottle of water and left the room. She paused at the pantry. *No way, sister. You are turning into a human garbage disposal.* "Love you, Dad," she called over her shoulder. "Please let yourself out."

The next morning, Anne dropped by Randy Vers' office. She was anxious to share the information her study-buddy Bryan had found.

Randy was thrilled. "This certainly proves Sherman is lying about revenues. I will have the subpoena prepared for Mr. Statton immediately. That should shake things up."

"It doesn't help with Stephanie's murder," Anne said sadly.

"That's a matter for the police, Anne."

•••••••

The next few days at work Anne filled in for people who were out with the flu or on vacation. She was having trouble sleeping. She felt anxious and longed for a break in Stephanie's murder. It seemed that time was standing still. Nothing was happening. To make matters worse, Shane had warned her about interfering in his investigation and Maria had clammed up.

She looked forward to her mom's cookout and the chance to talk to Randy. She arrived at Jason's after class on Friday planning to spend the night. He had her favorite pizza waiting–the works with extra cheese and a chilled bottle of

Chianti. She was famished. She was barely in the door before she had devoured two slices of pizza, while standing at the sink. Jason put his arms around her waist, and kissed her neck. The uncorked wine sat on the table, untouched.

Anne woke up Saturday morning feeling fully satisfied. Making love with Jason was more than just sex. It left her feeling contented–and loved. She reached over to caress Jason–no Jason. She opened her eyes and stretched, sinking deeper into the mattress. She then pulled the covers up to her nose. She heard Jason puttering in the kitchen and smelled the coffee. She felt relieved that she did not have to get up and rush to work. Jason came in and handed her a cup of coffee. He sat next to her and gently caressed her leg. His hand moved up her leg. She set her cup on the bedside table and pulled Jason to her. The coffee could wait.

The day was warm and sunny. Perfect for a cookout. Jason and Anne took separate cars. She needed to go to the law library afterward. She pulled up in front of her mother's house and parked behind Randy and Ilene's van. Jason parked behind her. Anne's mom met them at the door. She showered them with hugs and directed them to the back yard. Randy tended to the chicken on the grill and Ilene played ball with their two young sons, Billy and Jimmy. Anne went to the bar and poured a glass of wine. Jason grabbed two beers from the cooler and took one to Randy. Anne relaxed in one of her mother's wrought iron lawn chairs.

Ilene walked over and took a seat next to Anne. "Those two boys of ours will be the death of me," she said with a grin.

"They are active," Anne said. "I don't know how you do it."

Ilene fumbled with her wine glass. She appeared nervous. "Anne, has Randy told you he has been dreaming about your father?"

"No, he hasn't. What kind of dreams?"

"He doesn't say, but he wakes up in the middle of the night and can't go back to sleep. It seems to have something to do with his frustration over the Sherman case."

"Randy and my dad were close. I know my dad thought of Randy as a son."

Ilene nodded. "I hear you had a problem with the Sherman transcript."

"Did Randy tell you about that?"

"He was concerned about you."

"I appreciate that. I appreciate the fact that he

saved my job. I'm just glad it's over."

"Get off your brother," Ilene yelled at Tommy. She left for a moment to break up the fight. "I just thought you should know about his dreams."

Anne nodded. *Dad, you've been busy.*

"Dinner's on," Anne's mother called. As usual, there was enough food for an army–and Anne's favorite chocolate cake for dessert.

After dinner, Anne saw Randy standing alone and walked over to him.

"We need a break on this case," Anne said.

"We sure do." Randy looked weary, beaten down. "We're running out of time. Judge Johnston has ordered us back into court. I can't stall any longer. The judge is no fool. He knows our case is weakened by Stephanie's death, but that's no reason to postpone any longer. I issued the subpoena for Mr. Statton and disclosed the information to Sherman's attorneys. No doubt they will claim an accounting error. It still doesn't pinpoint the location of the offshore account."

"I'm sorry I couldn't help any further. My frustration is with Stephanie's murder investigation."

"You've done a lot. And I appreciate your help. I think we're screwed." Randy gave a heavy sigh. "We're back on for Monday."

"What? That soon?"

"Afraid so. If we can't find Sherman's offshore account, Isabelle will never see a dime of it. I've failed her."

"I'm hoping the bastard is convicted of murder. I don't want him to enjoy his money. Not a penny of it," Anne added.

Randy smirked, "A weird payback, huh?"

Anne wandered into her father's law office. Nothing had changed. Piles of paper cluttered the large cherry desk. The bookshelves were packed with law books. Awards and commendations covered the walls. She walked around running her fingers over the books and memorabilia. *Why did you have to die?* A lump rose in her throat.

"You know, this was going to be our law practice when you finished law school." She turned. Her father stood by the credenza.

"Yes, I know," Anne said sadly. "I really looked forward to that." She could feel her eyes welling up.

"I didn't intend to die, you know. It just happened. I had so many plans for us, so many plans with your mother, and now it's—" his voice trailed off.

A huge sorrow washed over Anne. The room went silent.

"This can still be your law office. I would like that."

"We'll see, Dad," she whispered. "We'll see."

Anne glanced at the room, then left. She found Jason, Randy, and her mother sitting under the apple tree. Her father had planted it when Anne was a little girl.

"I hate to leave such wonderful company. Duty calls. I have to go to the law library."

Anne and Jason said their goodbyes. He walked her to her car.

"I'll see you later," she said. Jason took her hand and kissed it.

"Are you all right, Anne?"

"Yes. Just too many ghosts." They kissed and she drove off.

The law library was quiet and Anne was able to finish all her cases for the coming week in a short time. She looked at her watch—eight fifteen. Hard as she tried, she could not put Tim Sherman out of her mind. She had to be missing something. She felt compelled to go back to Stephanie Burke's. She needed to uncover evidence; the smallest piece would do. It was a nice evening. Someone had to be walking a dog.

Anne drove down the street and parked across from Stephanie's house. Not a soul was out. She waited. *So this is what surveillance is like.* She moved her seat back and stretched her legs. Her impatience grew with the passing minutes. A little while longer and she would go home. Unable to sit still a second longer, she crossed the street and crept to Stephanie's front window and peered in. Too dark to see anything. She walked around to the kitchen door. *This is where she was murdered.* Anne shivered, picturing the bloody scene. She tried the door. Locked, of course. Clark Meadows had double-checked when they left and wiped the doorknob clean of fingerprints. As if in a trance, she stood staring at the police tape hanging from the door. She heard something rustle behind her. Her heart jumped. She wanted to turn around. Instead she froze. *Probably a cat. Stay calm.*

Before she could move, someone slammed her against the door and pinned her to it. An arm reached around her neck and tightened. Something hard pressed into her back. She imagined it was a gun. *God help me.* Panic set in. *Ohmygod! I'm going to die!* Every time she budged, the grip tightened. She could feel hot breath on her face.

"Back off bitch," a man snarled into her ear. Pain gripped her. He held her neck so tightly she feared choking. "Do you understand me, bitch?"

She opened her mouth. Nothing came out. She managed to nod her head. *He's going to kill me.* She raised her leg enough to brace her foot against the door and pushed with all the force she could muster. *Damn!* He was too strong.

"Maybe I'll just finish you right now," he threatened in a gravelly voice. Anne let out a blood-curdling scream. He grabbed her mouth with his hand, forcing her head back. Her throat tightened. She struggled. She heard trashcans falling nearby. *Someone's heard me.* She grew braver. He turned to see what caused the commotion. The racket continued. The gun pushed deeper into her ribs.

"Next time won't be a warning." He threw her to the ground, knocking the breath out of her, and took off. She turned—the pain was searing—and saw him running across the lawn. A trash can lid caught him on the leg. A second lid seemed aimed at his head. He ducked, regained his footing and disappeared into the shadows. Anne lay still and tried to catch her breath. She shook from head to foot. *What have I gotten into?* Her legs felt like rubber. She struggled to get up then leaned against the door to steady herself. She was grateful to whomever had frightened away her attacker.

With one thought in mind–to get safely to her car–she fumbled for her car keys, dropping them twice as she crossed the street. With a quivering hand she unlocked her door. Once inside, she locked the doors, rested her head on the steering wheel, and took deep breaths. Slowly, her breathing returned to normal.

"Are you alright?" her dad asked. She jumped and screamed. Her knee hit the steering wheel and the horn blared. "Calm down," he said. "You're safe now." She turned to him and fell apart. He wanted to put his arms around her, try to soothe her. Rage replaced her fear.

"That son of a bitch," she screamed and pounded the steering wheel with her fists. "Sherman sent him. I know it." She continued her tirade. Then abruptly, the tears and fury stopped. She turned to her father. "Was that you who scared him off?"

Her father nodded. "Ghosts have some powers. All I could think of was to create a disturbance." The corners of his mouth turned up. "Not a bad shot for an old man."

Anne visualized her attacker sprinting across

the yard, dodging trashcan lids, and her body relaxed.

"Anne, Angel, it's important that you remember as much as you can while it's still fresh in your mind."

"Fresh!" she screamed. "I'd say it is damn fresh in my mind." She lashed out. "Did you just see what happened? I could be dead. I could be joining you."

"But you're not," he said softly. "And if you want to nail Tim, you have to remember details for the police."

Anne knew he was right. She ratcheted her rage down a few notches. Taking deep breaths, she began to process what had just happened. First, she wasn't dead. That was something to be grateful for.

"Let's go through some of the details," her dad said. She could tell by his flushed face and the concern in his voice that he was as angry and frightened as she was. He'd always been masterful at concealing emotion.

"Was it a man or woman?" he asked.

"A man."

"Young or old?" he pressed.

"From his voice, he sounded young, maybe in

his twenties." The details were starting to come back.

"What was he wearing?" She had to think clearly. All she could think of was his arm cutting off her air supply and his back as he ran away.

"He was wearing a dark hoodie," she said. The details came into focus.

"Anything else distinguishing? Think, Anne it's important."

"He had a southern accent. Definitely not from this part of the country." She felt more empowered.

"Now we go to the police." His tone left no room for arguing. Anne knew he was right, and she was glad for his presence and support.

"You know, Anne," he said softly, "I would never have let him hurt you."

"I know, Dad." A tear ran down her cheek. She wanted so much to be able to put her arms around him, hug him and have him return the gesture. Instead, they drove in silence to the police station.

The desk sergeant said Detective Maria O'Malley had the night off. Detective Shane O'Malley was covering. Anne paced in the waiting area. She had never been in a police station before. She eyed her company: an overly made-up young woman in a knit leopard print shirt that barely covered her navel and tight pink spandex leggings–she had to be a hooker.

"Hey, bozo," the young woman yelled at the desk sergeant, "where's my lawyer?" He ignored her. Anne wondered when Shane would show up. She was growing impatient.

"Anne, what's wrong? Are you okay?" Shane asked a few minutes later. He walked her to a small interrogation room. They sat across from each other at the cold metal table. One question and she began to cry. The words rushed out. Shane took notes. He wore a blank expression when he erupted. "You just couldn't leave it alone could you?" He was furious.

Anne was taken aback. She looked at Shane and watched his throat muscles tighten. His face went blood red. "Hey. I'm the victim here. I was attacked. Remember?"

"And would you have been attacked if you had stayed home? I don't think so." He slammed his notebook on the table and stood up. He kicked his chair. It went flying. Anne jumped. "Do you realize you could have been killed? Murdered just like Stephanie?"

"Shane, I'm sorry."

"Sorry? Sorry enough to risk your life? Sorry enough to risk this investigation? How sorry will you be if our case against Stephanie's murderer is thrown out because of you?"

"I just wanted—"

Shane opened the door. "We're done here. I have all I need." He turned his back on Anne and strode down the hallway.

Anne was devastated. Shane was her friend. What had she done? She looked around for her purse, then left the room. Her legs barely supported her. Tears rolled down her cheeks.

As she left the police station she noticed the young prostitute conferring with a man–her lawyer or pimp. Anne couldn't get out of there fast enough.

Unlocking her car she remembered Jason. *Oh shit.* He would be waiting and worrying. She had no doubt that Shane had called Jason by now. How was she going to explain this? She didn't feel ready to tell Jason about her father. Jason might think she was crazy. Still, until now, she had never kept secrets from Jason. No matter how nutty it sounded, she would have to tell him. How do you tell your husband-to-be that you're in cahoots with your father's ghost. Anne heaved a deep sigh.

When is the right time? She knew she had to come up with a good explanation.

CHAPTER

11

Jason paced the living room. Where was she? Shane had called him as soon as Anne left the station. He told Jason how she had been interfering with the investigation, snooping around Stephanie's house, and grilling a neighbor. And had been attacked. Dammit. She could have been murdered—just like Stephanie. Jason wondered if she falsified the transcripts. How far had she gone? He thought he knew her. Now he wasn't sure. He felt like he was losing his mind. *Where the hell is she?*

Anne parked. The lights were on in Jason's apartment. She felt a rush and longed for the comfort of his arms. She had not been able to come up with a plausible story for why she had been at Stephanie's house. Before she could put her key in the lock, the door flew open. Jason grabbed her, pulled her to him, and held her tightly.

"You impulsive idiot. What were you thinking?" He loosened his grip.

"I guess you heard?" she asked.

He sat down beside her on the couch. "Did you honestly think I wouldn't? Shane told me everything." Rage replaced relief. "Anne, when are you going to stop? You could have been killed. You may have jeopardized Shane's case in the Burke murder. I can't tell you how many ethical violations you may have committed." He felt frustrated and angry. He thought he would die if he lost her. He could kill whoever attacked her tonight. He put his head in his hands.

Anne had never seen Jason like this. The realization hit her that she had acted selfishly. She acknowledged that she might lose him. She hoped it wasn't too late to make amends. She vowed to never again become so self-absorbed. "I'm so sorry," she said. "Please forgive me."

"Just talk to me, Anne. What is going on?" Jason pleaded. "Don't you know how much I love you? I was worried sick."

She burst into tears. The words tumbled out. Anne spoke of her obsession with the case, her study group's help, the break-in, and her feeling of responsibility for Stephanie's murder. She even spoke about Randy's involvement. She stopped shy of divulging her father's part. She felt relieved at once.

"You broke into Stephanie Burke's house? What were you thinking?"

"Jason, I am so sorry. I never meant to hurt you."

He took her hands in his and kissed them. "We are quite the Miss Marple, aren't we?" The reference made her laugh and broke the tension.

"I guess I am." She slipped off her shoes. "Jason, I can't explain why this case is so important to me, but it is. I've got to make sure Sherman gets caught."

"Anne, do you realize you are interfering with the investigation? This is serious. Ohmygod, you were attacked."

Anne nodded. "I am so sorry."

"I accept your apology. You need to apologize to Shane. I have never seen him so angry.

"I know." She thought how she had involved her friends, had let them down. "I owe apologizes to a lot of people."

Jason went into the kitchen and returned with

a bottle of wine and two glasses. "You've gone off the deep end. We need to talk."

She sipped the wine, something red and fruity. She wanted so much to tell Jason about her father. But would he believe her now? Would he think it was an excuse? No, it had to wait. "Jason, I caused Stephanie's murder. My actions caused the death of an innocent woman. Can you understand how I feel? I'm responsible. I have an obligation to solve this. Does that make any sense?"

"Anne, stop blaming yourself. You had nothing to do with it."

"But –"

"No buts. It was not your fault."

"That's easy for you to say. I feel terribly guilty. And I can't shake it."

He caressed her hair. He sighed, "What can I do?"

She felt closer to him than ever.

"However," he continued.

"Uh oh," she said, "always a however."

"However, you have to promise that you will stop snooping on your own. This guy threatened you, hurt you. He wasn't kidding around. This isn't just my take. Maria and Shane agree."

"You're right of course."

"If I'm going to help, I need to discuss it with Randy Vers. But it seems like he is already involved." Anne flinched as Jason went to the phone. "I'm calling Randy."

She felt a tinge of remorse. How many people would she put in danger before Sherman was stopped?

"Randy, it's Jason. We need to talk. It's about Anne. She went to Stephanie Burke's looking for clues and someone attacked her. She's fine, but we need to wrap this up before it goes any further."

Anne's cheeks flushed. She felt invisible, like a little girl whose parents were talking about her—as if she wasn't there. She charged Jason's cupboard and tore through the snacks until she found some cookies.

Jason hung up and turned to Anne. "He's on his way over. And what are you doing?"

"Um Ubset," she mumbled through a mouthful of vanilla wafers.

"At least have some milk." He went to the refrigerator, took out a gallon of milk and poured her a glass.

"Tangs," she said as she gulped it down.

A few minutes later Randy burst through the door. He grabbed Anne's arm.

"How could you have been so stupid?"

"Hold it just a minute," Jason cautioned. "She's safe. She was trying to help. You're not innocent in this. You encouraged her to take part in this scheme." Anne and Randy protested. Jason cut them off. "There's more than enough blame to go around. Let's talk this through."

Over the next hour, they reviewed the facts. They had no proof against Sherman for the murder or the offshore account. The only solid evidence was tied to the attack on Anne. And they couldn't connect it to Sherman.

Jason glanced at the clock. "It's late. We've done everything we can for now. Anne needs rest. Let's call it a night."

Randy got up to leave and took Anne's hand. "Please don't go out on your own again. This is serious. Let the professionals handle it."

Anne half nodded. "Wait a second! I just remembered the Sherman case is on for Monday. Randy, I don't know how I can sit in the courtroom and look at him without losing it."

"Do you want me to get the Judge to replace you?" Randy asked.

She snapped. "Are you kidding? I'm not letting

this jerk get to me. I don't give in to threats."

She read concern in the way Randy and Jason looked at each other.

Randy left. Not ten minutes later Anne was fast asleep. Jason slipped in beside her. He couldn't sleep. What could he do to protect her? He didn't understand this obsession, but he knew it was beyond reason. There was something she wasn't telling him. It wasn't like Anne to keep secrets. He got up, poured himself another glass of wine, and spent the rest of the night in the chair watching Anne sleep.

The next morning Anne pulled on jeans and sweater. She turned to find Jason standing in the doorway. His jaw was tight.

"Jason, what's wrong?"

"I know we discussed this, but I am fearful for your safety. Is there anything I can say to get you to abandon this obsession of yours?"

"You know better. I am committed. I promise to be more sensible." The minute she used that word she knew it was a mistake.

"I think you passed sensible a long time ago." He started to say something more but threw up his hands in exasperation and walked away from her. "When you're ready to tell me what is really going on, I'm here." He shook his head and walked out.

Anne was speechless. How could she tell him that her father's ghost was the driving factor? It sounded ridiculous. But she had to do something to win back Jason's trust. She had to fix this. And soon.

She found Jason in the kitchen. "Jason, you're right. I am so sorry. I wasn't thinking." His back was to her. "Can we please talk about this tonight?" He didn't respond. "Jason, talk to me." She went over to him, placed her hand on his arm. He turned to face her. He looked sad, defeated. She put her arms around him. "Can you ever forgive me?" Jason put his arms around her.

"Anne, I don't ever want to lose you. Promise me you won't do anything crazy like this again."

She didn't say the words he wanted to hear. But she promised herself that she would be more careful in the future.

•••••••

Anne dreaded Sunday and facing Maria in study group. Anne knew she had overstepped her bounds and may have jeopardized the case. She hoped that, out of friendship, Maria would forgive her. She approached Maria, whose look reminded her she was in deep trouble. As if she needed a reminder.

"Don't even bother explaining, Anne. No matter what I said, you've played amateur sleuth on your own. I think you see what that got you. I've given up trying to talk sense to you." She turned away.

"I'm sorry, Maria. Really. I've learned my lesson. It won't happen again. Can you forgive me?" Maria's face softened.

"Only if you promise to let us do our job."

"I will."

"I can't tell you how serious this threat may be. And I can't protect you if you keep interfering."

"I understand."

"Okay then, enough said. I will share one tidbit of information provided you don't go off."

"Tell me," Anne begged.

"We have some substantial leads that may wrap up this case."

"You—"

Maria held up her index finger. "This means you back off and let us do our job."

Anne promised. *Tim Sherman is going to get his.* She couldn't wait to go into court on Monday, look Sherman in the eye, and know his days are numbered.

After study group, Anne went home. She had hoped her dad might be there, but there was no sign of him. She felt disappointed and sad. She had come to look forward to their time together. She grabbed a bottle of water and settled on the sofa with *Time* magazine. She couldn't wait for Monday to arrive.

•••••••

Anne was awake before her alarm went off. She arrived early at the courthouse. She stepped off the elevator and waved to Shirley Williams, who waved back before disappearing into Courtroom B. Anne collected her supplies and headed for Judge Johnston's courtroom. Gerard was already there. He sashayed over.

"I guess we are back on. The Judge wants to wrap this up. The delay has wrecked our schedule."

Anne knew what he meant. The docket had to be moved back and other judges had to cover. No one in the system liked this kind of disruption.

Randy walked over to Anne.

"You okay?" he asked with concern in his voice.

"I'm fine, Randy. Really fine. I hear it from confidential sources that they may be close to an arrest." She nodded toward the defendant's table.

"No kidding." He looked perplexed. "Well, it doesn't tell us where he hid the money. So my client does not benefit. Except to satisfy her thirst for revenge."

Isabelle Sherman came in with the other attorneys from Randy's firm. Tim Sherman and his entourage trailed. Anne thought he looked a little remorseful. "Just wait," she thought. Tim was head to head with one of his attorneys.

Gerard, satisfied that all parties were present, called the courtroom to order and the Judge appeared.

Randy called Isabelle Sherman to the stand. Through teary testimony she recounted how she had helped her husband build the business. She said they had used her money to get started. Randy narrowed his questioning. She testified that, over the last few years, large sums had been systematically removed with no explanation.

Next, a string of accountants testified that it was highly irregular practice. Mr. Statton testified to the fees he had paid Sherman's firm. Sherman's attorneys had an excuse for every claim. Accounting errors, reclassification of income, unallocated expenses. Despite all the testimony, there was no evidence linking Tim Sherman to an offshore account. Just sloppy accounting.

Judge Johnston announced a recess for lunch. Anne had hoped to meet Jason for lunch. But he left a message on her cell phone that he would be tied up until one o'clock or later. She could tell by his voice that he was still upset. She didn't like leaving things unresolved. She grabbed a sandwich and went back to her office to eat and check e-mails. At twelve forty-five, fifteen minutes before court was to convene, she heard shouting outside her office and recognized Tim Sherman's voice.

"I'm tired of all your bullshit. Get your butts back into court and get this divorce settled. You and I both know they can't pin this on me, so let's get this case wrapped up. I want to get on with my life."

"I know, Tim," his attorney answered, "but it's not that simple. You and I both know the police have nothing on you for the murder. They told us that. But this is a different issue. Judge Johnston is a different breed. I don't think he believes your story about the money. He may look for a way to structure the settlement that remedies that." The attorney sounded apologetic.

"There is no evidence! There is no money trail!" Tim snarled. "Just get it done–or else. Do you understand me?" Menace filled his voice.

When Anne heard them walk away, she left. She saw Sherman walking toward the courtroom, his attorney cowering behind him. *No evidence against him. What did he mean by that?* Her stomach knotted.

Testimony ended quickly. Without Stephanie Burke or other proof, Sherman was right–his wife's attorney had nothing. Two more accountants testified. It was clear there was no trail to follow. By three, both sides had finished. Judge Johnston announced that he would have his decision by the following Wednesday. Court was adjourned. Anne collected her papers and glanced at Randy, who appeared despondent. Randy would not be able to secure for his client more than normal alimony and a property settlement.

Jason walked in. "Sorry I couldn't do lunch."

"Not a problem. Let's get a beer. I need a breather."

Jason put his arm around her waist. "I do love you."

"I know you do."

•••••••

Tim Sherman sat back in his leather chair, feet on the hassock. He sipped the double-malt scotch and drew on his fifteen-dollar Cuban cigar. *I fooled them all.* His face was a picture of self-congratulatory smugness. His attorneys had told him he was free to travel as the police did not consider him a suspect. *I did it. No reason to stick around for the judge's decision. I already know what it will be. Isabelle won't get one thin dime.*

12

Anne felt the stress leave her body as she waited for the court's ruling. She rolled her head back and forth–no pain. The knots had vacated her shoulders. Her stomach no longer ached. Her new pencils were intact. The Sherman case was over. The only missing piece was the judge's decision. But that was out of her control. *Finally I can put it behind me. Move on.* She knew that Jason was right. She had been overly stubborn and behaved badly. She had allowed her obsession with the case to create divisiveness in their relationship. She would make it up to Jason—or die trying.

But Stephanie Burke's murder was another issue. That she could not dismiss. It haunted her day and night. Disappointment engulfed her that no new evidence had turned up. She felt powerless, a failure.

"Hey, doll face," Gerard called to Anne. "I have something I know you're dying to see." He waved a paper in her face.

"Is that the judge's decision?"

"It certainly is." He wore a devilish grin. Anne grabbed at the paper. He snatched it away.

"You can read it when the attorneys do." He bent over and whispered, "I can tell you this: Mr. Sherman is going to be happy and Mrs. Sherman is not."

"You're teasing me. That's not fair!" Anne protested.

"No, it's not," Gerard continued, "but what are you going to do? Without finding the money–which we both know exists–all the judge can do is divide the money he knows about."

"Unfortunately, you're right." Anne heard footsteps and turned in time to see Tim Sherman's attorneys. She averted her gaze. She couldn't stomach looking at them and walked toward Courtroom B for a personal injury case. On her way she bumped into Randy as he stepped off the elevator.

"Randy, I—" He held his hand up, cutting her off.

"I know, I know. Not a good day for my client."

"What was your first clue?" Anne asked. He smiled, but without mirth. Her dad would not be pleased either, but she had done everything she could do. Where was her father? She hadn't seen him since the incident at Stephanie's house. Anne missed him. She needed his support. It seemed she had alienated everyone she cared about. She needed her Dad's assurances that her efforts had not been in vain. Dammit. *Dad, where are you?*

Unable to control herself a moment longer, Anne caved after class and pulled Maria aside. "I know you told me to trust you, and I do. But I can't let this go. It's so damn unfair. Tim Sherman is getting away with cheating his wife out of money that is rightfully hers. Please tell me you are about to nail him for Stephanie's murder." Maria's expression told Anne that was not going to happen. Anne's stomach turned over. "Are you saying he's going to get away with it?"

"Anne, he has an air-tight alibi, and our investigation is going in a different direction."

Anne felt her knees go weak. She lowered herself into a chair. *Oh no! This cannot be true.* "Maria, you can't let this man get away with—"

"Anne, stop this. Stop it now! We will find Stephanie Burke's murderer, but it is not Tim Sherman." Maria walked away.

Anne felt furious. Her temples pulsated. Her teeth clenched. What would it take to convince them of Sherman's guilt? Her thoughts jumbled and she felt light headed. She had to go somewhere quiet and think.

Opening the door to her apartment half an hour later, she smelled her dad's pipe smoke. *Thank God.* "Where have you been?" she said to an empty room. She found him at the kitchen table. She didn't give him a chance to reply. "They have nothing on him. He is getting away with it. We have to do something." Her eyes filled with tears of frustration. "Everyone hates me. Oh Dad, I'm so upset."

"I know Anne," he said calmly. "But I have a plan."

"Thank God! Now we can do something. I am tired of sitting by while that sonofabitch gets off scott free." She took a deep breath. She would do whatever it took to prove to the police that Sherman was guilty. "Tell me. What can I do?"

"After you were attacked, I decided to watch Stephanie's house to see if your attacker would return. I had a hunch."

"Did he?"

"He did. I watched him snoop around the house and then break in through a bedroom window. He carried out a computer. I followed him. He's staying at a cheap motel on the south side of town. As of a little while ago, he was still there."

"Let's go," Anne cried, grabbing her purse.

"Hold on a minute. What are you going to do? March into his motel room and accuse him of a crime? We need to lead the police to him. You stay clear. He is dangerous and I don't want you anywhere near him." her father cautioned.

"We can't wait. What if he gets away?"

"Anne, I told you I have a plan. But it involves you."

"Anything."

"This is what I propose. Call Shane and tell him you broke your promise; you went back to Stephanie's. You saw the man that attacked you and he was breaking in. Tell Shane you followed the intruder to the motel. Tell him you're at the motel. That should get some action."

Anne grabbed her purse and turned to her father, "Shane, Maria, and Jason are going to collectively kill me, so we can't mess up. You coming? Let's bring this guy down together."

"I'm with you all the way." Anne called Shane's cell phone from the car.

"Shane, this is Anne. Are you on duty?"

"Yeah, I'm at the station. Why? This better be about Trivial Pursuit."

"Well, not exactly." She could sense from Shane's audible breathing that he was not pleased.

"What do you mean by 'not exactly?'" His words were pointed and deliberate.

"I drove by Stephanie's to see if I could recognize anything that would help you identify my attacker."

"Anne. That's the final straw. I don't care how good of a friend you are, I'm having you arrested. Jason will thank me."

"I know, I know. But hear me out. I saw the guy that attacked me and he was breaking into Stephanie's house."

"Get out of the area. I'm sending a squad car."

"Shane, listen to me. He loaded the car and drove off. I followed him to the Shady Pines Motel on the south side of town. He went into Room 206."

Shane was furious. "Anne, for the love of

God, stay put. Don't leave the car under any circumstances. He attacked you once. He will do it again. We're on our way." The line went dead.

Anne turned to her dad. "That went well. He's on his way. He's going to kill me, but he's on his way."

Anne drove to the motel, dimmed her lights and pulled slowly into the lot. Her dad pointed to a room on the second floor, halfway down the low-slung two-story building. "That's his room. His car's over there." He pointed to a rundown Ford Fairlane.

She kept her eyes glued to 206 and saw the lights go out in the room. A moment later the door opened and someone came out. Anne squinted but could not make out his features. His size and gait told her it was a man, wearing a hoodie just like the one her attacker had worn.

"Damn," Anne said, "I think he's leaving."

"Let me handle this. You stay here. Lock the doors and don't leave the car. Do you hear me?" her father warned.

Anne nodded. She watched as the man walked down the exterior corridor and down the stairs. *Where is Shane?* Anne's skin started to crawl. She began to wring her hands. They felt clammy. *He's getting away.* He reached the parking lot and walked toward his car. Anne's stomach knotted. *He can't get away. This is my only chance. Where is Shane?* She fought the impulse to confront him and watched as he took out his car keys. *I have to do something. Sherman is not getting away with it.* She put her hand on the door handle, unlocked the door and inched it open. The interior light went on. Anne pulled the door shut and slumped in the seat. *Damn. Damn. Damn.* Anne felt so stupid. She raised her head just enough to see the parking lot. The man had stopped. He looked toward Anne's car. She crouched behind the steering wheel. *Please don't let him see me.* She was afraid to look again. She had no idea where he was. *Ohmygod. The door's unlocked.* She cursed and slid her arm up to the lock. She froze as footsteps approached her car. Her heart raced. Perspiration beaded on her forehead. She didn't dare move. Or breathe. She listened. Silence. She took a breath. *Thank God he's gone.* She remained crouched behind the steering wheel, still as a statue.

The door sprang open. The man grabbed her arm and dragged her from the car, screaming. "I told you to back off, bitch!" With her right hand, Anne held tight to the steering wheel. Her fingers ached. The man yanked her left arm again and she landed face down on the asphalt. A sharp kick to the ribs knocked the wind out of her. She tried to crawl away. The best she could do was to roll on her back. When he tried to kick her again, she grabbed his leg. But he broke free. He grabbed her hair and slammed his fist into her head. Pain seared through her. She thought she would throw up. Anne covered her head with her arms and waited for the next punch. She heard footsteps moving away from her. She opened her eyes and watched him running toward his car.

"What the hell," he yelled. "Get away from my car!" Anne heard glass shattering. It sounded like someone had taken a bat to the headlights and taillights. But who? She didn't see a soul other than her attacker. Plastic and glass continued to fly everywhere.

"Where are you, you coward?" he shouted into thin air as he circled the car. "Come out you bastard," he screamed. More glass flew. This time it was the windshield that shattered. The driver's window followed. He pulled out a gun and started firing wildly, "I'll kill you, you bastard!"

Anne snapped to her senses and crawled behind her car. Sirens blaring, two police cars screeched into the parking lot. Four officers jumped out, guns pointed at the attacker.

"Drop it. Get down on the ground," one of the officers ordered. Her attacker dropped his gun and dropped to his knees.

Anne rose with difficulty and, leaning against the car, inched around it. Her legs were rubber. Her head hurt. Her ribs ached. She was shaking.

Shane ran over. "Are you alright?" You look awful. We need to get you to the hospital."

"I'm fine. A little shaken up." Anne watched as an officer handcuffed her attacker.

"What you gonna do about my car?" he was shouting. "That bitch vandalized me. What you gonna do about her?"

Anne flinched. "Shane, he is the one. He's the one that attacked me."

"He's in custody now. You're safe," he assured her. "I'm calling Jason. We'll discuss this later–at the police station." He didn't sound happy.

Anne longed for Jason. Needed the comfort of his strong arms around her. She nodded weakly then started to cry.

Shane put his arm around her. He flipped open his cell phone and called Jason.

"Jason, it's Shane. Anne's with me—"

Jason jumped in. "Anne? Is she okay? Good God, what's she done now?"

"Calm down. She's fine. She may be under arrest, depending on my mood, but she's fine. But you better get here. She tracked down her attacker and it didn't go well. She's refusing to go to the hospital. We're at the Shady Pines Motel.

"I'm on my way." Jason was out the door and into his car before he finished his sentence. He didn't know who he was going to murder first–Anne, or the joker who had attacked her. Definitely her attacker. He could kill Anne later.

"Jason's on his way," Shane assured Anne. "What the—" He turned to see the prisoner break free and make a mad dash toward his car.

Detective Bridges caught him and slammed him against the car. The trunk sprang open. One of the officers walked around to the back of the car.

"Hey Shane, you may want to see this."

Shane ran over to the trunk. Inside was a bloody meat tenderizer.

"Well, I'll be," he said. "Read him his rights and book him on suspicion of the murder of Stephanie

---

Burke. Get him out of here."

The murder of Stephanie Burke? What was he talking about? Anne ran over to the car. "Shane, what's going on?"

Shane pointed to the trunk and the bloodied meat tenderizer. Anne stared in disbelief. She couldn't process it. She lost her balance. Shane caught her as she went down.

Jason arrived a moment later. Shane said Anne could fill out a police report in the morning. He decided he would not have her arrested. Jason took her to his house, cleaned her up and put her to bed. He sat close to her, stroking her hair until she fell asleep.

Jason watched as Anne slept. His feelings were mixed. He loved her with his whole heart, but he was angry that she had risked her life once again. Why was she keeping secrets? He was worried about her injuries. He looked at Anne's sweet face. Thank God she was alive and safe. Since they had caught Stephanie's killer, maybe now things would return to normal. She might even tell him the whole truth.

It took her a minute to realize where she was. The horror of the previous night came flooding back. Anne sat up. "Ouch!" Her ribs hurt. She wondered if she had a broken one. Her head throbbed and she ached all over. She had to sit on the edge of the bed to pull on Jason's sweatpants and shirt. She stumbled into the bathroom, wincing with every step. She peered into the mirror at her swollen and bruised face. *No concealer will camouflage this mess.* Jason came in and put his arms around her. When he caught her reflection in the mirror, he cringed.

"That's nasty. Are you sure you don't want to go to the hospital?"

"No, I'm fine, really. Just confused. Who killed Stephanie? Did Sherman hire him?"

"They don't know yet. Shane will keep us informed. Let's get you some coffee and breakfast. Shane will call when he knows something." Anne nodded. "I've called in sick for both of us."

"Jason, thank you for all the TLC. I'm so ashamed that I tried to keep things from you."

"Anne, I don't understand this, but I love you and trust you will tell me what's going on. If this relationship is going to work, we have to be honest with each other. We have to share everything: the good, the bad, and the ugly."

"I know. I know. Right now I need to rest." She

trusted Jason and knew she would have to explain everything when the case was settled. *I only hope he doesn't think I'm crazy.*

She stretched out on the sofa and Jason wrapped a blanket around her. She was sore and not relaxed enough to sleep deeply. She could hear the low hum of the TV and the rustle of newspaper pages. The news anchor reported the incident, but added nothing to what Anne already knew.

Feeling somewhat better, Anne sat up. "Jason, we have to put these pieces together. I can't be wrong about Sherman."

"Randy called while you were resting," Jason said. "He's dropping by. Let's go over everything again." He grabbed a legal pad from his desk. He listed each piece of information Anne relayed, drawing lines between related items. Nothing connected Sherman to the killer.

"Maybe Sherman hired a contract killer," Anne offered. "I hope Shane and Maria can break him. I wonder, why haven't they called?"

"They will."

The doorbell rang. Jason made a dash for the door. "Hi, Maria."

"Speak of the devil. Do you have any news?"

Anne asked.

"I have no idea why I'm even talking to you. I must like you a helluva lot. So I'm going to tell you what is going on. This will bring closure to this case and your escapades."

"Why? Did that punk admit Sherman hired him?"

Maria ignored the remark and sat next to Anne. "You're a mess. Maybe a doctor should look at you."

"I'm bruised but I'll survive. I want to know what you found out. That's something that will make me feel better."

"First, Jason, got any coffee?" Jason brought Maria a mug of coffee and sat down.

Maria spoke slowly and deliberately. "I am not going to waste my breath telling you how stupid you were." Weakly, Anne protested. Maria ignored her. "The perp we apprehended last night was Stephanie Burke's twenty-two year old nephew."

"Nephew?" Anne was shocked. "That's not possible."

"It is possible and it is true." Maria continued. "He has a drug problem. He needed money to support his habit. He came up here to get money from his Aunt Stephanie. He was searching her house for money when she came in and surprised him. They fought over money and struggled. He grabbed the meat tenderizer and killed her."

Anne ran her fingers through her hair. She had trouble wrapping her mind around Maria's words. "No. I'm sure you're wrong. Sherman hired him to kill Stephanie."

"Anne, we have a confession. He doesn't even know Tim Sherman."

"That's what he says. He's lying. Keep questioning him. Make him break."

"Anne, listen to yourself. Stop this." Maria placed her hands on Anne's shoulders.

"Anne, darling," Jason stepped in, "listen to Maria. Sherman didn't murder Stephanie."

Anne felt devastated. "Sherman goes scott free and gets all the money? It's not fair." Anne went limp. Her dad's mission had been a complete failure.

"Anne, Sherman didn't kill Stephanie. He had nothing to do with her murder. He didn't get away with anything as far as Stephanie is concerned. I don't know what can be done about Sherman's offshore account. That's not the Homicide Department's business. That's for the court and

Mrs. Sherman's attorney."

Anne sat in disbelief, questioning herself. *I am such an idiot.* "How could I have been so wrong?" she asked Maria.

"First, might I remind you that I told you not to—"

"Jump to conclusions," Anne interrupted.

"That's right, but without your help we may never have found the nephew."

"What do you mean, without my help?"

"Remember when you described the young man that assaulted you?"

"Yes, but—"

"You said he had a southern accent?"

A light bulb went off in Anne's head. "So that's what led you to her nephew."

"We had the local police in Alabama check on the nephew. It turns out he had gone missing. He became a suspect after your assault. But we had no idea where he was or how to find him. Stubborn you found him, complete with the murder weapon. If the trunk hadn't popped open when it did, we might still be looking. Odd, isn't it?"

Anne realized that it was not at all odd. She knew her father had had a hand in it.

"I'm not going to hug you. I don't want to add

to your pain. Take care of yourself. I will see you in class."

"Thanks for putting up with me. You're a great friend."

"You're welcome. You redeemed yourself."

When Maria had gone, Anne turned to Jason. "I have been such an idiot. How could I have been so obsessed? I let Sherman get to me. It all stems from something my father instilled in me when I was very young, watching him in court. When he felt he was right, nothing would stop him. I inherited his sense of justice. That's why I felt responsible for Stephanie's murder. I needed to expose her killer. I know it's something my father would have done."

Jason put his arm around her. "Anne, darling, we were all caught up with this. Everyone thought Sherman murdered Stephanie. Don't be so hard on yourself. Let it go."

"If anything good has come out of this, it's that I no longer feel guilty. I know I wasn't responsible for her death."

Jason held her close and she snuggled against him. "At least you are safe and it's all over." His touch soothed her. "When you are ready to talk, I'll listen."

•••••••

Tim Sherman heard the news from his lawyer. *So it was that good-for-nothing nephew.* He had always advised Stephanie to stay away from that trash. But she always felt she could help him. Oh well, her bad luck. He picked up his plane tickets. Soon he would be on a sunny beach with his millions. He smiled as he poured another scotch. He lifted his glass in a toast to himself. *Life is good. Yes indeed, life is good.*

13

Anne and Jason ordered her favorite fully loaded pizza for supper. They needed a quiet relaxing evening.

"I'm still in shock over Stephanie's nephew," Jason said. He dished out the pizza.

"Don't remind me. I'm so glad I can put this mess behind me and focus on law school. No more playing amateur detective."

"Thank God for that." Jason picked up his wine glass and tipped it to Anne. "To you, my darling. No more detective work."

The doorbell rang, interrupting Jason's toast. "That must be Randy," Anne said. She opened the door. Randy enclosed her in a massive bear hug.

"Not too tight. My ribs hurt," she said.

He backed away. "Oh, I'm so sorry. I didn't mean to hurt you. You look awful."

"I'm fine, Randy. Just a little stiff. Thanks for the compliment."

"You know what I mean," he blushed. "I'm so glad you are safe. Why would you do such a stupid thing?"

"I thought he could lead us to Sherman. I was wrong."

"You did lead the police to the nephew–and the murder weapon. That's huge."

"It doesn't help your client. I wish we could have caught her husband with the goods."

"You can't win them all. I'm just thankful you are okay."

Jason piped up, "Enough talk about the Shermans. Have a piece of pizza."

"Don't mind if I do."

Despite Jason's protests, Anne left in the morning, citing a need for clean clothes and time alone. So much had happened over the last twenty-four hours, her head was spinning. She needed to talk to her dad. Jason agreed to drive her to her car, then he followed her home to make sure she was safe. Anne kissed him goodbye at the door. "I'm fine," she said. "Please don't worry." The familiar smell of pipe tobacco greeted her.

"Hello, Angel."

"Hello, Dad." She felt elated. She wished she could rush into his arms the way she had done when he was alive. Instead she settled for blowing him a kiss. "I am so glad to see you. I really missed you." She sat on the couch and kicked off her shoes.

"What a strange chain of events."

"I'll say." They sat in silence.

"I'm so sorry we couldn't expose Tim," Anne offered.

Her father nodded thoughtfully. "Oh, I almost forgot, Randy will be calling you. I think you will be pleased." He drew on his pipe.

Anne looked at him quizzically. "Randy? I just saw him last night."

The phone rang.

She picked it up. "Hello, Randy."

"How did you know it was me?"

"Just a hunch." She winked at her father.

"You will never believe what I have in my hot hands."

"The morning newspaper?"

"No. I went into the office this morning. Sitting on my desk was a letter from Stephanie Burke."

"What?" Anne exclaimed. "No way." She

motioned to her father. He wore a smug expression as he puffed away. "Why would she have sent you a letter—and what does it say?" Anne thought she'd jump out of her skin waiting for Randy's reply.

"She was so furious with Sherman over his infidelity, she decided to get even. She sent me all the information on the offshore account. I mean *all.* It's in the Bahamas. She gave me the phony company name, all the account numbers, and all the passwords. Anne, this is incredible."

"Ohmygod, Randy. I can't believe it. We've caught the bastard." Anne looked at her dad who was grinning from ear to ear.

"Now Isabelle will have access to all the money that Tim hid."

"I'm thrilled. But why did it take so long to get the letter."

"I guess it got misplaced in the mailroom. Someone must have found it and put it on my desk. I sure wish I could thank whoever it was. Go figure."

"Go figure," Anne replied as she looked at her accomplice. He shrugged his shoulders as if to say *it's all in a day's work.*

She said goodbye to Randy and turned to her dad. "Aren't we proud of ourselves."

"Well, quite honestly, I am. I couldn't stand

Tim getting away with cheating Isabelle."

"You certainly performed a miracle."

"With your help, Angel. With your help. And don't forget that."

"And we helped to solve Stephanie's murder. If I hadn't been so obsessed with Tim, Stephanie's nephew might have gotten away with it."

"We're quite a team. Move over Nick and Nora."

The phone rang. "Yes, Jason." Anne listened for a minute. She shrieked. "You are my hero. Go get 'em." When she hung up she clapped her hands. She wished Jason were there. She would have hugged him until he begged for mercy. That would have to wait until later. She turned to her dad. "That was Jason. He spoke to Randy and he is on his way to court to get arrest warrants for Tim. He says there's enough evidence to nail Tim on fraud, conspiracy, and perjury charges. He said Tim is not going to enjoy the contents of his offshore account for a long, long time–if ever. I am so excited." Her dad's steely resolve broke and he laughed uproariously.

A feeling of sadness clouded over her. "Does this mean I won't see you again?"

Her dad put his pipe down. "You're not getting

rid of me that easily, Angel. I plan to be here for you for a long time. You and I have a special bond. I intend to see you graduate from law school, pass the bar, and take up practice in *our* office. I will dance at your and Jason's wedding, and I'll marvel at my wonderful grandchildren. No, I'm not going anywhere."

Tears filled Anne's eyes. "I love you so much, Dad. I'm glad you'll be around."

"I can't leave. We have work to do. A lot of new cases are in the pipeline. I was looking into one the other day—" His voice trailed off. Anne rolled her eyes. *I better enroll in a self-defense class ASAP.*

"Oh?" Which case was that?"

•••••••

Tim Sherman held tight to his passport, boarding pass, and briefcase. He had forty-five minutes to kill before his plane's departure. While watching the takeoffs and landings, he congratulated himself for pulling it off. Isabelle was no longer his problem. And Stephanie's nephew had conveniently taken care of his other roadblock. He could look forward to sun, sand, and a lot of beautiful women. Lots and lots of beautiful women. *Yessiree, life was good.*

From the corner of his eye he spied two police officers heading his way. He looked around to see where they were headed. In seconds they were facing him, hands on their guns.

"Mr. Tim Sherman?" Detective O'Malley asked.

"Yes, I'm Tim Sherman. What's wrong?"

"You are under arrest for fraud, conspiracy, and perjury. Will you kindly come with us?"

"No, I won't come with you. There must be some mistake. You can't detain me. I'm boarding a plane in a few minutes. I'm calling my lawyer." Sherman reached in his jacket for his cell phone.

O'Malley grabbed Sherman's arm, thrust it behind his back, and cuffed his wrist. A few seconds later he cuffed the other wrist.

"You can't do this to me. Do you know who I am? Who is your superior?" Sherman's face was red. The blood vessels in his neck stood out like a bas-relief.

Detective O'Malley tried to suppress a grin. "You have the right to remain silent—"

ABOUT THE AUTHOR

"I have always loved writing. When I was a child, I wrote short stories about a meddling skunk who insisted on 'saving the day' for her fellow woodland creatures. There was not a big calling for such a heroine in the small farming community of Iberia, Ohio, where I attended high school. So I became practical and obtained a BS and MBA in Business and a law degree. Now that the practical stuff is out of the way, I have returned to my first love—writing mysteries. Being a mature grown up, I have replaced Sarah Skunk with a meddling ghost. Makes sense to me."—Jacqueline Fullerton.

Jacqueline Fullerton is a successful businesswoman and attorney in Columbus, Ohio, where she lives with her husband, Tom, and dog, Flash.